Deep & Crisp & Even

Alan Grainger

Also by Alan Grainger

The Tree That Walked
The Klondike Chest
It's Only Me
The Rumstick Book
The Learning Curves
Father Unknown
The Legacy
Blood On The Stones
Eddie's Penguin
Deadly Darjeeling

Amazon Edition

ISBN 978-1475105889

For
Hannah, Ben, Emily, Sam,
George, Charlotte, Jack,
And, as always,
Maureen.

It is always the best policy to speak the truth,
unless of course you are an exceptionally good liar.

Jerome K F Jerome.

Templederry, County Tipperary, Ireland. Thursday 12th November 2009. 2.45pm.

He left the car in the station car park, crossed the road to the corner of Main Street ignoring the black and white stripes of the town's only pedestrian crossing and proceeded to walk slowly up the hill past shops mostly unchanged since he was a boy. When he got to Meath Street he turned into it and headed for the Garda barracks, a police station there since the time of Queen Victoria, a cut granite building which had once withstood a siege and which in a strange way was symbolic of the citizens of Templederry - unsure whether it should move forward with the times or remain anchored in the past. A cast iron seed merchant's weight which hadn't been used for its original purpose since the 'metric' came was holding the door open.

He entered; it was cool and dark inside. A policeman in his shirt sleeves was sitting at the only desk, his back to the counter. By the stripes on his epaulettes he appeared to be a sergeant. 'It's yourself then.' he said. 'And you'll be here for the key I suppose, give me a minute.'

'My God … Mattie … I'd forgotten you'd joined the Gardaí. How on earth did you know it was me?'

The sergeant swung round, a huge grin on his face. 'Aha! I saw you going past the window, and anyway I was half expecting you, I heard you were on your way.'

'You must have been speaking to 'Fatso' then, I rang him from London.'

'Jesus, don't call him that.'

'Why not? He'll always be 'Fatso' to me, same as you'll always be 'Mattie' - they're just names. And I tell you what … I can see us now: you, and me, and Fatso, and Jimmy 'O', the 'bad boys' of St Catherine's. What was it Miss Hennigan used to call us - 'The Unholy Alliance' - Jeez, we must have made her life a holy hell but she drummed something into us didn't she, set us on the right path? D'you hear much of the others these days?

The sergeant gave a little upward nod. 'Fatso, I see him; Jimmy's in Australia getting rich. Here.' he said, throwing the man a key with a label tied to it by a piece of string. 'Are you alright for a lift?'

'Yeah I'm fine I brought the car; I'll be here for a week … maybe more. There'll be a lot to do.'

'Nasty business … especially with him being down there on his own.'

'Will there be an inquest?'

'What … with an 'accidental death?' You can bet on it. It'll be a week or two though.'

The man nodded, pocketed the key and went out to his car. Four miles to go, 'four country miles' as his father used to say, and he'd be at the place where he was born - the farm where he'd first seen light, where he'd spent his first twenty years - the prison from which he'd escaped when he'd eventually taken matters into his own hands and headed for England.

He'd only been back twice since: once for his father's funeral twelve years back, and once five years before that again after his mother died; duty calls to show respect he didn't have for people he didn't love. The present visit to bury his brother, his only sibling, would be the last he'd ever make. Once he'd tied up the loose ends and sold the place for whatever he could get for it he'd have cut his last link to the place - a miserable little farm on the boggiest land in Tipperary, an ugly stone building surrounded by rusty roofed sheds sitting in the middle of a handful of soggy fields.

He could never understand why first his parents and then his brother had stayed there so long, why they hadn't sold up and moved on. No wonder they'd a chip on their shoulders, no wonder they were always miserable. He was glad he'd escaped the fate awaiting him should he have inherited it, couldn't imagine how he'd have coped if he'd found himself tied to a life and a place he couldn't bear, imprisoned by both until he was too old to think of, let alone *do*, anything else.

Driving through Scarna he realised he should have bought milk and bread before he left Templederry. 'Ah well never mind I'll get what I want here.' he said to himself, slowing down at the little shop attached to Monkey Mooney's garage at the end of the village. There was no-one in the place he could see when he went in, other than an overweight balding man of his own age. He was wearing a brown shop coat and leaning on the counter squinting short-sightedly at the front page of the Nenagh Guardian through a magnifying glass.

'Where's the milk?' the man asked him, moving along the line of shelves opposite the counter. 'and I'll be wanting …'

The bald headed shopkeeper straightened up and blinked before taking one hand from the counter top and running it lightly across the top of his head to check the straggle of carefully coiled hair; then he sniffed and wiped his nose with the back of his hand. 'Milk is it?' he said, 'It's in the fridge at the end alongside the cheese and butter. There's no bread if you're looking for that. He'll be here again in the morning if you're …'

'What about crackers?'

'Cream crackers? Yes, we've got some of them. There's been run on bread today though. It's the weather.'

'Really, the weather?'

'People on holiday, they're all wanting bread for sandwiches. Can't keep up with 'em … are you on holiday?'

'No I'm here on family business.'

'You're not Irish?'

'Well I am as a matter of fact.'

'You don't sound it.'

'I've been away a long time.'

'If you came from round here you'll see plenty of changes and there'll be more when they start on the new road.'

'What new road?'

'The Lake Drive. Big job. Bord Failte - the Irish Tourist board … they're behind it.'

'Is there a *need* for a new road?'

'Of course there isn't … but there's a demand for it!'

'Is that so?'

'Oh yes … particularly from those lucky enough to have a frontage on the lake.'

'Why? Ah … I see … yes … worth a few bob.'

'You have it in one.' said the shopkeeper. 'Anyone with access to the lake'll make a fortune if they hang on a bit.'

'Ah yes - the old 'ransom strip' - I know what you mean.' said the man, approaching the counter with a carton of milk, a block of cheese, and a packet of Jacob's Cream Crackers.

'Yes, if you've got one of them and you've held back you're in the driving seat. Got everything you want?'

The man nodded. 'More than I was expecting get to tell you the truth, if what you say's correct. How do I find out more about it … the road I mean?'

The shopkeeper sniffed again and tapped the counter. 'It's in the paper … I was just reading about it.'

'Ah … the Guardian o'course. I'll take one.'

'There's a load o'stuff inside about the road and the rest of the County Development Plan, and there's maps, proposed routes … the lot. I was looking at it when you came in.'

'That's me, then.' said the man, dumping his purchases on the counter.

The shopkeeper smoothed out the newspaper he'd been reading, folded it, added it to the pile of biscuits, cheese, and milk, the man had picked out, and then punched up the till. 'That'll be six, sixty five.' he said.

'And you'll have bread tomorrow?' asked the man, as he counted out the money.

'Don't come early; he won't be here 'til ten.'

The man smiled and picked up his purchases. 'I'll be here at ten on the dot.' he said, walking towards the door.

'Wait a minute.' the shopkeeper called out 'I know you don't I? You're poor old …?'

But the man didn't hear him; he was outside the shop and reaching for the door handle of his car.

Three Months Later

The Old Deer Park, Fyling Castle, Fylingford, Sussex, England. Monday 15th February 2010. 9.58 a.m.

Betty Burgess didn't spot it at first but Ringo did, and he dropped to the ground snarling though bared teeth. She checked to see what had caught his attention. It was a red shoe, a woman's red high heeled shoe, and it was stuck toe down in the snow.

'Oh no you don't Mister,' she said, 'you're not bringing that back,' and turning to her husband, contentedly puffing on his pipe as he plodded along behind her, added: 'You'll have to do something about this wretched dog of yours, Clive.'

'What?'

'Ringo, he's found something.'

The man took his pipe from his mouth. 'So what d'you want me to do about it?'

'Oh for Goodness's sake, he wants *that.*' she said, pointing to the shoe.

Clive turned and straight away saw what Betty had missed … inside the shoe there was a foot, and it was attached to a leg which was sticking out from under a deep drift of snow which had built up against a stand of young hawthorn bushes. 'God Almighty, Betty.' he gasped, 'Ringo's found a body.'

Sussex Police Major Incident Suite, Sussex House, Brighton Sussex. Monday 15th February 2010. 9.58. a.m.

Detective Chief Inspector Foxy Reynard had been at his desk since eight. Detective Sergeant Lucy Groves and Detective Constable Norman Best, the other two members of his team, sat opposite to him. They'd been 'in' since half seven to clear their desks before heading for his office and the Monday morning 'catch up' meeting. The only excuse he'd ever accept for either of them not being there, and on time, was if an emergency cropped up.

At ten o'clock exactly he looked at his watch, smiled, and took up the coffee jug. Before he got as far as pouring from it though D.C. Best pulled a packet of Chocolate bottomed Hobnob biscuits from his pocket, and with a big smile on his face offered it to Reynard who put down the jug and opened the top drawer of his desk. It was crammed to the top with unopened similar packets. 'Ye - es ' he said, drawing the word out with heavily staged wisdom, 'the stocks do look a trifle low!'

Sergeant Groves raised an eyebrow; she could see at least twenty packets. 'Come on, Guv!' she chided, as she began to return a packet she had in her hand to her handbag. You've enough to feed the proverbial five thousand there.'

Reynard's eyebrows shot up in an assumed look of shock. 'Hang on, hang on.' he said, leaning across the desk and grabbing the unexpected contributions. 'I've another drawer for presents … and anyway what d'you mean by 'enough'? You've seen the procession of scroungers who waltz in here every time I come into the office; these'll all be gone by the end of the week, trust me.'

'They'll be gone alright Guv but who'll have eaten 'em that's what I'd like to know?'

'Thieving policemen … who else!' Reynard replied with a grin, opening one of the packets and passing it round.

Such pantomimes are part of the ritual performed every Monday morning - a few light hearted moments and a laugh or two before the week gets under way. And there's always a decent cup of Costa Rican coffee and a Hobnob biscuit to be had. The whole building is aware of what goes on in Reynard's office on Monday mornings and takes advantage of it. Foxy Reynard is as well known for his liking of coffee and biscuits as he is for pursuing villains … and that's saying something.

In truth he's a stickler for regular order of every sort, frequently exasperating his colleagues by rigidly adhering to fixed ways of his own, including the establishment of proper chains of responsibility, the pooling of information, the avoidance of duplication, and …most important of all … rigid adherence to agreed plans. On top of everything else he's a devil for protocol, insisting on addressing everyone by rank and surname only unless he happens to be alone with them. Some officers, especially the younger ones, think he's old fashioned - freakish even - and they're inclined to make fun of him. But they have to be careful, for while he's undoubtedly 'old school' he's also the most successful detective in Sussex.

Reynard would stand out in any crowd: a slightly rotund straight backed fifty year old man of presence with a head of close cropped grey curly hair and a disarming smile. He's generally dressed in a well-tailored well pressed dark grey suit, under which he wears a cut away collared white shirt and a Paisley patterned tie. (Constable Best reckons he probably wears one in bed!)

However, if he appears to be old fashioned and out of step as far as dressing and ad-dressing, is concerned, he's bang up to date with everything else. He assesses every new technical advance and adopts it as soon as he's mastered it - assuming it's compatible with his aims. Anyone who aspires to be on his team, and there are plenty who do, has to keep abreast of what's going on or perish. He doesn't mind contradictory views in debate or discussion; indeed he encourages both as a means of winkling out the truth. But he won't tolerate insubordination, won't have a maverick on his team. If you're 'with' Foxy ... you're 'with' Foxy ... and that's that. Despite his exaggerated meanness with his biscuits for which he's notorious he's actually a very generous man ... even his detractors concede it. And as mentioned he always sports an engagingly disarming smile, even though he may be a long way from laughing.

His 'right hand man' is thirty-six year old Detective Sergeant Lucy Groves. She's a slick dresser too and also favours dark coloured suits. In her case they're relieved and feminised by clever choices from a rack of subtle coloured silk shirts and lamb's wool pullovers she has in her bedroom. Her blonde hair, which is always arranged to look casual, is in truth skilfully and expensively styled to produce the soft waves which flop about her face. Mentally as sharp as Foxy, she's just as competitive; but she's more subtle, and eschewing the 'full frontal' mode of questioning which *he* alternates with long periods of tension building silence, *she* generally adopts a more oblique approach. They make a perfect pairing regarding which Reynard is ambivalent for, happy as he is to see her fast progression as a result of applying the skills he's taught her, he fears they'll eventually take her away from him.

To that end he's grooming the third member of the team - Detective Constable Norman Best, - a bright young twenty five year old copper with the build of a second row forward and the sharpness and wit of a cockney barrow boy. He wants to get on, and he's willing to learn. 'Norman' to his mother and the D.C.I, when they are on their own, he's 'Next' to D.S Groves and everyone else 'in the job'.'

'Right,' said Reynard, putting down his mug and running his tongue across his lips to savour the last chocolate coated crumb. 'You first Sergeant … let's have a quick appraisal of where we are in the cases we have on hand. Afterwards D.C. Best can tell us what the other teams're up to … OK?'

Groves nodded and shook back the hair from her eyes. 'We've a few 'on the go' at the moment Guv, and they're all near the final report stage. I've a draft ready for the one on the 'Miss Per' from Angmering - the eighteen year old who ran off after telling her boyfriend her father hit her whenever he got in from the pub and …'

Reynard rocked back on his chair and closed his eyes, 'Yeah, yeah, yeah ... with her mother looking on and frightened to stop him, yes I remember. Anything new come in?'

'The boyfriend got a card from her yesterday; he left a message on my answer phone saying he's bringing it in this morning. She's OK apparently; she's got a job in Coventry and sharing a bed-sit with a girl who works in the same supermarket.'

'Right; you've checked her age, haven't you?'

'No, I did.' said Best. 'Got it from her mother and confirmed it with her school records.'

'And it's ...?'

'Eighteen … eighteen last month.'

'Good. See what the postcard says when he brings it in then Sergeant, and if you can get an address or any sort of a contact, even the name of the Supermarket the girl works in, you can get the local station to send a W.P.C. round to make sure she's OK. If she is … wrap the whole thing up.'

'And the parents?'

'Parents? Let 'em stew, it was them who drove her away … right, if you've nothing else on that one what else have you?'

'Not much. We're still ploughing our way through a mountain of paperwork looking for unlikely movements in the personal bank accounts of two members of the staff at PharmoChem … you know … the 'missing drugs' affair. I was going to get D.I. Crowther to help with the financials if that's OK? … D.C. Best and I are well out of our depth.'

'I'll have a word with him, he owes me one.'

'Right ... that's all I have then. Oh yes, I was going to try get rid of the last few bits and pieces we have on Nelson Deep's murder; the appeal's failed.'

'Fine … archive them. And, er …what about the pilfering at the Princess Eugenie Hotel, you never said a 'dicky bird' about it?'

'I'm still interviewing.'

'OK. You and Best stick with the Eugenie, I'll continue with the arson at Century Cabs. Is that all then?'

'Yes, Guv, it's pretty quiet compared to what we usually have on our plate. As a matter of fact I was thinking of asking if I could take some leave … I've a quite a bit owing.'

Reynard nodded and opened his eyes again. 'Sure, why not? We can talk about it when we're finished here. Right, your turn Constable Best - what's the rest of the division up to this morning?'

'Well they're certainly not up to their necks, Sir.' said Best, 'D.I. Crowther's lot are focussing on the girl who was strangled on the race course - Julie 'Someone'. They haven't got far; they're still looking for witnesses.'

'I'll ask him if he wants any help when I talk to him about the money trail at PharmoChem which has you and Sergeant Groves stumped … a 'quid pro quo'.'

'A quid pro? Is that a financial term Sir?' asked Best who, on seeing the look of amusement on the faces of the other two immediately wished he'd kept his mouth shut.

Reynard shook his head; he didn't approve of silly remarks, and with a coolness Best felt added. 'Really … I see ... and have they just the one job have they, Crowther's lot?'

'Everything else has been put on hold … orders from the top I believe. Cut backs.'

'Oh not again! And D.C.I. Saunders's team?'

'They're all out today … the body on the railway line … remember… the one found last week near Preston Park.'

Reynard gave a slight nod. 'Ah yes … another girl wasn't it? Did you say you knew her Sergeant?'

'I pulled her in a couple of times … Amy Faucette. I felt sorry for her to tell you the truth. She had a terrible life at home, ran away at sixteen and went into prostitution to survive. Some punter'll have done for her I expect; I hope he's caught.'

Reynard edged a piece of wheat husk from between his teeth with his finger nail and flicked it over his shoulder. 'I expect Saunder's squad are concentrating on their murder and Crowther's lot'll be doing the same on theirs.' he said, 'Could they be connected … the deaths of the two young girls - the one on the race course and the one on the rail tracks?'

Best, drumming his finger tips on edge of Reynard's desk for which he got a black look, shrugged his shoulders.

'What's the matter … in a hurry are you?' asked Reynard.

'No Sir … not at all … I was thinking.'

Before Reynard got the chance to reply Groves took up the point. 'They might be, Guv - both girls' looked as though they were dressed for business, if you know what I mean, but our boys will have thought of that already surely?'

'Yes they probably have … but sometimes you can't see what's staring you in the face. Anyway ... if there's nothing else we'll knock it for today.' said Reynard, standing to signify the end of the meeting. 'And don't forget your time sheets … both of you ... and your expenses for January … they have to be in by the end of the week.'

'Excuse me Guv' said Best, suddenly leaping from his chair and rushing for the door. 'I've just seen D.I. Crowther walk past. 'If I don't grab him now while I've got the chance he'll disappear again.'

'Go on then.' said Reynard 'Jaldi.'

Best stopped and swung round. 'What?'

'Jaldi ... it means 'hurry' in Hindi .... Oh ... go on you'll miss him.'

Best, still bewildered, nodded and raced off.

Reynard watched for a moment in silence and then walked over and closed the door. 'Stay where you are Lucy,' he said, when he saw Groves was about to get up from her chair. 'We'll not get a better chance to talk about this leave you want.'

'Oh, great.' she replied, 'I suppose there's no chance of two consecutive weeks. I need sunshine … the snow we've had lately is getting me down.'

'I'll check the diary.' said Reynard, reaching for the telephone which had started ringing.

The Old Deer Park, Fyling Castle, Fylingford, Sussex. Monday 15th February 2010. 10.12. a.m.

Clive Burgess folded down the lid of his mobile telephone and handed it back to his wife. 'They're on their way - fifteen minutes. If you wait here I'll walk down to meet them.'

'I'm not staying here on my own Clive, someone might come and we're not supposed to be in the park. I knew we oughtn't to have ignored the sign and pushed through the hedge. You hang on with the dog - *I'll* go back to the car. Who am I looking for anyway?'

'How should I know, they didn't say? But there'll be some policemen and an ambulance probably. I told them we were parked just outside the East Gate and that we'd been exercising our dog in the park when he spotted the body.'

Betty nodded and set off on the quarter mile trek back to the car, which she could just see outside the chained up gates. As she walked, she scanned the trampled snow of the footpath and the unmarked surface either side of it. What she expected to find she wasn't sure - something the girl had dropped possibly - but there was nothing. And then as she got nearer to the big ornate wrought iron gates she heard the distant sound of a siren.

Clive in the meantime had been looking around too. There were no footsteps in the snow near the body, other than his own and the dog's, so it must have been there all night with the snow gradually building up and drifting over it. He wondered who the woman was and how she'd got there. Had she been murdered on the spot or killed somewhere else and dumped there? 'Thank God I don't have to sort that out … or tell her family.' he thought.

As he stood pondering it started to snow again - fine white flakes swirling this way and that in a freshening cold breeze. He looked hopefully down to the East Gate. In the distance he thought he could just make out Betty, she was nearly down at the gap in the hedge. 'Go on woman … hurry up for Christ's sake;' he shouted. 'I'm bloody-well freezing up here.'

Barely had she disappeared from his sight when Ringo, who'd been standing quietly at his side, spotted the shoe again and lunged forward. The unexpected movement practically brought him down. 'Stop it you silly damned idiot!' he yelled; but the dog ignored him and continued to dart backwards and forwards at the end of the tightened lead. Clive dragged him back to his side again and looked down to the gates … still no sign of any policemen or paramedics. As he swung back he noticed Ringo had stopped barking and was looking at something behind him. Before he got a chance to swing round to see what it was though, the dog leapt forward again and all but brought him down with the lead wound round his legs. As he struggled to regain his balance he saw what had caused the upset. There was a man with a black and tan Jack Russell terrier coming down the path towards him from the West Gate, he was laughing his head off. 'Got yourself in a right old tangle there mate, haven't you?' he said, when he got near enough to be heard. 'Hang on … I'll grab the dog if you let go the lead … what's been going on?'

'Don't start me.' Clive answered. 'Damned animal's gone bonkers.'

'Why … what did you do to him?' the man asked as his little Jack Russell, having spotted the bright redness of the shoe, began to yap.

'You may well you ask … he's found a body,' answered Clive, 'over there … where the shoe is. Wife's gone to meet the police … they're on their way now.'

As he spoke, they heard the siren.

The man nodded. 'That's an ambulance. Want me to do anything? If not, I'm off. I only came to exercise the pooch.'

Clive shook his head. 'No … you go.' he said, and began walking down to meet two policemen he could see coming towards him through the blizzard.

'Alright Sir,' said the first officer when they got up to him. 'Thanks for waiting but we'll take over now; you can go down and stay with your wife. One of us'll be down shortly to take your names and addresses; we just need to check what's been going on here first. Fifteen minutes tops and we'll be with you. Can you wait that long?

'Of course we can.' said Clive.

In the end it was nearer twenty before one of the policemen came back down to note down their details and tease out from them how they'd found the body.

'D'you know who she is?' Betty asked. 'Was she murdered or what?'

The policemen gave her a smile and shrugged his shoulders. 'We don't know any more than you do luv. We checked her temperature and she was frozen stiff as a board - no sign of life at all.'

'So what happens now?' asked Clive.

'Not much until S.O.C.O. gets here - that's the Scene of Crime Officers. When they're on the job we back off and C.I.D take over. You'll be able to go once they've spoken to you, provided you don't mind hanging on. They won't be long; you can wait in your car.'

'I hope they hurry up my teeth are chattering.' Betty answered, shivering and drawing her coat tighter around her to emphasise the fact.

'And I'm ready for a stiff one.' replied Clive, taking a card from his wallet. 'Here you are … it has our address on it.'

The policeman nodded. 'Civil Engineer eh?'

'A retired one.' Clive answered, 'We'll wait in the car until your pals have finished with us.'

'Yeah, go on … get in out of the cold.'

Betty climbed into the front passenger seat but before Clive had got as far as putting Ringo in the back, the S.O.C.O. vehicle drew up. Ringo went berserk. He broke away from Clive's grip and leapt at the S.O.C.O. car's window, barking and scratching so aggressively he frightened the wits out of the young policewoman driver who sat behind the wheel with her face in her hands.

Clive grabbed Ringo by the collar, dragged him back, and shoved him in his car before turning to the policewoman and smiling an apology. He only got a half-hearted response from her but the man in plain clothes sitting beside her, Sergeant Geordie Hawkins, winked and gave what could easily have been taken as a smile.

Sussex Police Major Incident Suite, Sussex House, Brighton Sussex. Monday 15th February 2010. 10.31. a.m.

Sergeant Groves was still trying to juggle her diary to create a window for her holiday when D.C.I. Reynard came back from the briefing. 'Put that away Lucy and find D.C. Best.' he said, as soon as he saw what she was doing. 'Something's come up and I need you both in here pronto. We've got what looks like a murder.'

'Right, I'm on my way.' Groves replied, stuffing everything she'd laid out in readiness for her holiday talk into her briefcase and going off to look for Constable Best. She found him talking to Detective Inspector Crowther about the money trail he was trying to uncover in the PharmoChem case.

'Come on Next,' she said, 'Sir wants us and he's in a hurry; looks like we've got a murder as well.'

'Hope it's not ours' said Crowther, 'I've put a lot of work into tracking down Julie Fitzgibbon's killer.'

'I don't think it is.' Groves answered.

'It'll be Amy Faucette then, D.C.I. Saunder's case.'

'Not her either. The Governor just came back from a meeting in the Super's office and he was all fired up. I reckon it's a new one entirely. Come on, he's waiting for us.'

When they got back to his office Reynard was on the telephone. 'Yeah, yeah, yeah … but I thought the place was closed up for renovations. Oh OK … and have S.O.C.O been called in? … Right … who? … fine … OK … and has the doc' been informed … Oh he's gone over already, excellent … and it's Doctor Moss, better still … OK, we're on our way.'

As he put the telephone down, Groves and Best spotted the twinkle in his eye. 'Right, listen up.' he said, and he began reeling out the information staccato fashion: 'A woman's body was found about half an hour ago. It was discovered by a couple walking a dog in the park up at Fyling Castle. It's mostly buried under the snow apparently, only her foot could be seen. S.O.C.O. are already there and Doctor Moss's on his way. OK? We leave in ten minutes … my car … any questions? No? Last cup of coffee then, it'll be cold up there in the snow.'

Groves looked out the window at the flakes floating past and nodded, but Best was already thinking ahead. 'Just a minute Guv, Fyling Castle's closed at the moment … they're doing it up. I saw it in the paper … National Trust.'

'So what … maybe someone thought with no one around it'd make it a good place to hide a body. Come on, who wants coffee, I won't ask again.'

'Have we time?' asked Groves.

Reynard laughed. 'I doubt if the victim's in much of a hurry.'

The Old Deer Park, Fyling Castle, Fylingford, Sussex. Monday 15th February 2010. 11.00. a.m.

By eleven Reynard Groves and Best were trudging up through the swirling blizzard and approaching the tent which was flapping about in the wind as the S.O.C.O. team tried to erect it. Doctor Gordon Moss the police surgeon - a forensic pathologist and 'Mossy' to his friends - was there before them. He was looking grim faced as he held the tent frame at one end having arrived at the same time as S.O.C.O. and been co-opted to help erect it.

The white overalled Scene Of Crime team leader, D.S. 'Geordie' Hawkins, an old friend of Reynard's, fought his way out of the partially erected structure when he heard their voices. 'Thank God you're here Foxy' he said, 'we could do with a bit of help. Here grab hold of this and watch where you tread … especially where I've pegged it.'

Reynard took the loose end of material Hawkins handed him and passed it to Best. 'I don't do tents.' he said, sticking his hand in his coat pockets. 'So … what d'you make of it from what you've seen?'

Hawkins brushed a snow flake from one of his eyelashes. 'It'll be tasty Foxy … right up your street I shouldn't wonder … but I'll have to dig her out first … she's almost completely covered.'

Reynard didn't answer; he was looking down at the ground and frowning. 'Is this how it was when you got here then … all flattened down like this … all the footprints obliterated? How the hell am I supposed to establish what happened when you guys have …?'

'Keep your hair on' Hawkins fired back. 'There were only the finder's footprints and a few belonging to his dog when I got here. He and his wife were up here walking the animal. They're in their car down at the gate unless they've gone home; one of the 'uniform' boys has their address. We've identified all the tracks and footprints leading to where the body is and the whole lot were photographed as we moved in. You can take it from me … there were no footprints around here other than the ones I've mentioned. Mind you there could have been others under the top layer; it's being snowing on and off for hours.'

As they spoke the tent had been taking shape and was almost secured. 'Right, OK … that's fine ... only I thought.' said Reynard, struggling to stifle a censure. 'Can we go in now?'

"Look in' only at the moment if you don't mind. We're about to remove the snow to see who we've got.'

'Young or old, d'you think?' asked Best.

'Don't know yet. I haven't seen anything above her calf.'

Reynard rubbed his hands together to warm them and nodded. 'We'll be back in half an hour then.' he said.

Hawkins waved dismissively but Reynard went on speaking. 'And in the meantime we'll have a sniff around outside to see if we can spot anything.'

Geordie Hawkins laughed. 'You'll be lucky it's been snowing all night, four inches or more and it's still coming down.'

Reynard didn't hear him, he and his two companions were already dividing up the area they'd decided to search first: Groves was to walk back and look around the car park at the East Gate, Best was to do the same at the West Gate, while Reynard was to walk the full length of the footpath between the gates searching as he went.

Only Groves came across anything of possible consequence - a woman's blue and white right hand ski mitten. She found it squashed into the snowy ground in the car park near the gap in the hedge. It must have been run over by a vehicle which was there after the first heavy snow fall of the previous night but before the later much lighter one which had only partially covered both the vehicle's tyre tracks and the mitten. 'If it *was* the victim's and you're *right* with the timing, it may have been the couple who found the body who ran over it.'

'Anyone get their name?' asked Reynard.

'Burgess: Clive and Betty, local.'

'Right.' said Reynard, 'it doesn't matter if they did run over it it's the only thing we have … so bag it.'

'D'you want us to check all the tyre prints before they thaw or get covered up?' asked Groves.

'Are there many?'

'Plenty down at the bottom end where our car and the S.O.C.O. van are; a few more by the gate where I found the mitten and some way up at the top end of the car park.'

'Check the lot.' Reynard replied. 'Photograph them if you can, sketch them and measure them if you can't. Try and work out the movements of every vehicle which came in or out of the car park and see if you can find the order in which they arrived and left. In the meantime I'll go back up and check to see if the doctor's got anything for us yet.'

As Groves and Best made their way back down to the car park, Reynard returned to the S.O.C.O. tent.

Hawkins was well advanced with removing the layers of snow covering the victim. Even so, Reynard couldn't resist prodding: 'Oh, God! You haven't got far … I thought you'd be done.'

Hawkins, on his hands and knees, turned his head immediately. 'You'd be the first to bloody-well complain if I rushed it Foxy so shut up.'

'Alright, keep your hair on,' Reynard replied. 'When'll you be finished? Because if I were you …'

'If you were me mate you'd tell me to bugger off, so shut up and let me get on with it. Every bit of snow has to be removed with care so we can tell if there's anything between her and the top surface. There's a hard crust under the new stuff and with a bit o'luck I'll be able to work out when she was put here.'

'Okay, Okay, Okay … we'll push off and come back when you've got her uncovered - you can ring me. I suppose it *is* a woman … from the shoe?'

'Or some guy who's got his lines crossed … I still don't know … but it looks like it.'

'Has Doctor Moss gone?'

'Mossy? Oh yes … said he was cold … as if I wasn't! He's done a runner down to the Three Pigeons, the pub opposite the University. Said he was going for a coffee but he'll be knocking back something a bit stronger if he's running true to form, know what I mean?'

'I might as well join him … Half an hour?'

'Give me a break there's only two of us here. Make it an hour.'

'Fair enough … an hour.' said Reynard, ushering Groves and Best out of the tent. 'Pity we came in the one car,' he said, 'we'll have to stick together now so we might as well all join Doctor Moss for coffee. But you're not to have any fortifying additives to it … comprendo?'

Best said nothing - he was still learning; but Groves smiled.

Brighton Police station
John's Street, Brighton Sussex
Monday 15th February 2010. 11. 05 a.m.

Marion Palfrey stood at the glass window looking into a room full of Policemen and Policewomen sitting at desks writing or telephoning, and then she pressed the bell marked 'Press'

Woman Police Constable Jane Carville put down her pen, went over to the window, and slid it back. 'Can I help you?'

'I'm not sure … maybe I'm being paranoid.'

'About what?'

'Someone might be missing but I'm not sure.'

'I see.' said the W.P.C., summoning up a friendly smile. She'd seen hesitancy before when a person unused to talking to the police lost their tongue the first time they needed help. 'Well,' she said, 'who's gone missing for a start?'

'A work colleague of mine; I was to meet her at her place last night. We were going on a job together at the Phoenix Gallery … a new exhibition of paintings and sculpture … but she didn't turn up. And I was to meet her again this morning in the office … but she never appeared there either. I waited outside her flat for well over half an hour last night but it was so cold I gave up and went home.'

'Didn't you try ringing her or texting her?'

'Yes of course I did but I got no answer. I mean I probably wouldn't have been so worried about it if it hadn't been for those two girls getting murdered recently, and I … well … I expect it's nothing … it probably isn't. Maybe I'll wait a bit longer. Yes I'll do that, I'll see if she contacts me and if she doesn't I'll come back in the morning. Sorry for troubling you.'

'Wait a minute Miss,' said Carville, when Marion turned and started back towards the door. 'Why don't we get down a few details while you're here and then if you're still anxious tomorrow we'll have everything on hand … just as a precaution like … you know … we'll be prepared.'

Marion stopped as the policewoman spoke, and returned to the widow. 'Are you sure?'

'Sure I'm sure … it won't take long. I'll get The Daily Report Book and we can do it in the waiting room. It's over there behind you. You go ahead and take a seat I'll join you in a few ticks.' said Carville, who went in with the book shortly afterwards. 'Right then, let's start with your name and address.' she said.

When the girl's own essential details had been recorded Carville asked her to give a few details of the friend about whom she was worried, and to more fully explain the reason for their proposed meetings.

'I'll try.' Marion replied, 'Her name's Rosaleen Sommerton, most people call her Roz and we're both with The Globe. She's self-employed but under contract to the paper as the Brighton area correspondent and features writer. She acts as though she's the manager but she's not, she's just bossy. I'm the local news assistant: weddings, funerals, school sports days, that kind of thing; and there's another girl who sells advertising space. The paper's Head Office is in Horsham as you probably know, we just have a one room office in Brighton; it's the same in Lewes. We're at 112, Old Worthing Road, over a chemist's shop. I happen to live nearby at 63, so it's handy. I'm in a bed sitter. Roz's place is in Jutland Street, Number 3A. It's the ground floor flat of a house just along from The Feathers Hotel on the seafront.'

'The Feathers … I know it … a swanky place.'

'I've never stayed but I had a meal there once. As a matter of fact the article we're going to work on next: 'Eating Out In Brighton', is going to include a piece on The Feathers Hotel. We were supposed to start our research there this morning but Roz never turned up at the office or sent a message to say why. And she's still not answering her phone or her door. I went round earlier; got a lift from my boyfriend.'

'OK, back to last night …?'

'Well, we were to get together at her place to plan our approach for today's job at the Feathers Hotel. We were to do it before we went to the Phoenix Gallery. I got there, sometime after seven as she'd requested - she said she couldn't make it earlier because she was going out somewhere … but she wasn't in when I arrived and there were no lights on. She didn't answer her mobile 'phone or her door bell either; I tried both. It was the same this morning; I even tried tapping on the window but … nothing. Her car was parked over the road from her flat last night and it was still there when I went round today. I went to the Gallery on my own in the end and I half expected her to turn up late, all apologetic. But she didn't appear at all. I left eventually at about ten and took a taxi home.'

'She lives alone from what you say?'

'As far as I know she does but she has a lot of boy-friends, she's always out. I sometimes think she's engaged. She used to wear a ring on her engagement finger but it wasn't an engagement ring if you know what I mean … no diamonds or rubies or sapphires or anything like that. But not a plain one either, not like a wedding ring, it's sort of like a flower made out of gold. I was going to ask her about it last week when I noticed she'd didn't have it on but I chickened out; she can be quite sharp - she's got a real temper.'

'She's not married anyway?'

'No I'm sure she isn't - she might have a partner; I've heard he mention a man called Geoff, she might live with him.'

'May be *he* lives with *her*!'

'Yes maybe, but I doubt it and I've never seen him whenever I've been at her flat. I don't know much about her personal life really when I come to think about it, except she's always 'on the go': parties, weekends in France, holidays in Portugal, dinner in all the posh places. She moves in some very fancy circles way above my level. Mind you it *is* her job I suppose … picking up tittle tattle and so on. Her mother lives in Upper Beeding, and she once told me her Dad had left them a long time ago. I don't think she has any brothers or sisters.'

'Or children?'

'Children … Oh I never thought of them. No I can't imagine her with kids.'

'So her life's all fun and no responsibilities?'

'You'd think so … but she's not happy.'

'What makes you think so?'

'I'm not sure. I just an impression I get … she's forever trying to force things to happen, nudging people … you know what it's like … and when they don't, she sulks.'

W.P.C. Carville leaned back in her chair and yawned. 'Sorry - late night.'

'I know what you mean.'

'No, no … working. I didn't get away until well after ten, I'd been on twelve hours. OK … that's all very comprehensive Marion, no wonder you're a reporter. I'll just check over …'

'Here, you won't tell her what I've said will you?'

'No not a word. Now … let's see if I've missed anything.' Carville replied, scanning the page to check what she'd written. 'Ah yes, her phone number - do you know it?'

Marion took a small pocket note book from her handbag and read out a landline number, a mobile telephone number, and an e-mail address. 'What happens now,' she asked. 'do you send people out to look for her?'

'Eventually we might, but I shove all this stuff over to the Major Incident crowd in Sussex House first; they decide what's to be done.'

'I'm glad I stayed; I nearly didn't.

'It's always better to play safe Marion, that's what I say. Now if you can give me a description of your colleague I'll attach it to what you've told me, and in next to no time we'll have dozens of people looking for her. So let's start with age.'

'Thirty seven she says; she dresses younger but I think she's older.'

'Build?'

'Slight and around five five in height; light wavy hair down to her shoulders; eyes ... oh dear … I don't know … I can tell you she usually wears trousers though, not skirts, and they're often tucked into knee length black suede boots. Last week she had a ski jacket on and mittens - blue with a white flash. If she's not at home she's probably got them on. She's a very modern woman … confident, d'you know what I mean? She makes me feel inadequate.'

'No surely not.'

'Oh yes she does, and she seems to have plenty of money … more than she'd get from the paper. She needs it too because she has very expensive tastes in clothes and perfumes, not to mention her car … and she takes these marvellous holidays as I mentioned. She went to Dubai recently and that's not cheap; and Madeira.'

'Did you say the car was outside her flat?

'Yes … oh you should see it, it's an Audi Quatro.'

'Is it? Ought I to be impressed - I don't know much about cars. Anyway, Marion, that'll do for the moment. I'll put all this into the right hands the minute you've gone but you must promise to telephone me if she turns up, we don't want to waste time looking for someone who isn't lost.'

Marion was hardly out of the front door before Constable Carville was at the front desk talking to the duty Sergeant. 'I think you should see this, Sarge,' she said. 'it looks as though one of Brighton's high flyers has gone walkabout.'

The Three Pigeons,
Lower Road, Fyling, Sussex.
Monday 15th February 2010. 11.08 a.m.

Reynard sat opposite Doctor Moss in the middle of the room sipping from a cup of coffee. Groves and Best had coffee too but they were a little way off doing their own thing … which in her case was making a shopping list for things to be picked up before she went home … in his it was reading a report of the previous Saturday's Brighton and Hove Albion football match against Wycombe Wanderers which had been abandoned at half time because of the weather.

'What's that you're drinking Mossy?' asked D.C.I. Reynard, when he saw the strange concoction in the glass the doctor had before him. It looked and smelled like whisky, a hefty measure of it, but it had a slice of lemon spiked with cloves floating in it and it was steaming.

'Hot whisky. Best thing on the planet on day like this.' Doctor Moss replied, reaching for a handkerchief. 'You can take all the medicine you like Foxy, but this is the stuff if you've a cold coming on.'

'Ah … an ancient cure passed down to you through generations of the Moss family.'

'It's not a cure Foxy, it's a preventative. My favourite treatment for any ailment … better than the best drug ever made. Why don't you try one?'

'Not me, I'd probably fall over. Anyway I don't like whisky much, I prefer rum.'

'Do you? Well make it with rum if you like; it'll be just the same by the time you get the gubbins in.'

'The gubbins? Oh yes I see, the lemon and so on. Yeah, maybe … now what about this body … are you likely to have any problems because of the snow?'

'Time of death d'you mean?'

'Yes … will it affect your calculations?'

'It might; but then again it mightn't.'

'How d'you mean?'

'I was thinking about this when I saw the crime scene. It all depends on whether the death took place up there or somewhere else. If it was up there it must have been before the last snow fall because from what I could see.'

'You mean otherwise there'd have been more footprints?'

'Exactly.' replied the doctor. In which case I may get a better idea when I look at the state of decomposition - stomach contents and so on.'

'Yes … I see … but …'

'This really *is* the stuff Foxy, sure you won't change your mind?'

'It's too early for me Mossy, I'll stick to coffee. So let's get this straight - you've a good chance of working out when she died … I suppose it is a 'she' isn't it?'

'It's a 'she' all right, poor girl.'

'OK. So if she'd been lying on the grass and under the snow you might get one time of death, but if she's sandwiched in between the earlier and the later snowfalls i.e. put there sometime during the night, you might get another. Of course in neither case does it mean she died there. She could have been killed somewhere else and kept before she was dumped.'

'Of course she could have, but let's not worry about that aspect just yet.'

'Fair enough; I'll wait until after you've done your stuff in the mortuary. In the meantime I'd better get back up there to see how Geordie Hawkins is getting on.'

'I'll follow you up in a few minutes.' said Moss, taking another sip from his glass and savouring it for a moment before swallowing it.

The Old Deer Park, Fyling Castle, Fylingford, Sussex. Monday 15th February 2010. 11.55. a.m.

D.C.I. Reynard strode back up through the snow to the S.O.C.O. tent with Groves and Best. As they'd left the bar Doctor Moss had called out after them: 'Ten minutes Foxy, I'll be up in ten minutes.'

'Nearly there now.' said Hawkins, when they arrived. He was on his knees carefully brushing the last of the snow from the body with a decorator's paint brush. 'I'm just taking the last of it off Foxy. Sorry I've been so long but I'm on my own; my chap's gone for grub, we'll be here for a long time yet. What d'you think?'

Reynard, Groves and Best looked down at the body of a young woman wearing a dark blue loose fitting coat. She was lying face down on the snow. 'By the amount of stuff under her it looks as though she came here, or was brought here, sometime *after* the first snow fall.' said Reynard, who then turned to Groves. 'Get a tab on when it began snowing round here will you Sergeant … and find out when it stopped. You can go with her Constable.' he said to Best. 'This is important … ask around the area, and ring me as soon as you have something definite. Don't bother about weather reports; get the information first hand from locals. Right … off you go … be back in an hour.'

Once they'd left, Reynard edged round Sergeant Hawkins to take a closer look at the body. The woman was lying spread eagled on her front much as he'd envisaged when he'd seen the angle the shoe was pointing, but he could see very little else of her because of the long dark blue coat she was wearing. It was spread out across her body almost as if it had been arranged to hide her. In the same way her long hair, which he realised might be much fairer when it was dry, was covering not only the back of her head and neck but also obscuring her face. 'What d'you think Geordie, any sign of injury?' he asked Hawkins who, instead of answering the question, asked where Doctor Moss was.

'Still sipping whisky I expect; he says he has a cold. He said he'd be up soon. So … no obvious wounds?'

Hawkins shook his head. 'I can't really see much yet, and I don't want to touch her until 'Mossy' arrives, but so far … no. It might be a different story when we turn her over though. Want me to do it?'

'No, we'd better wait for him. What about the snow you took off her?'

'It's over there sitting in a pile on the plastic sheet. We didn't come across much of significance as we took it off though, so if there is anything there it won't be big. We're going to sift it later.'

'Fair enough; just peel back her coat a bit and see if you can spot anything.'

Hawkins caught hold of one corner of the coat and lifted it. 'She's got a red dress on and she's what … thirty five … thereabouts … can't see much else.'

'Pull her hair back so we can get a decent look?'

Hawkins was just reaching to do it when there was a roar from the entrance of the tent. 'Jesus! Don't touch her … I'll do it … but I'm not ready yet.' It was Doctor Moss, and he was exuding an aroma more to be associated with a distillery than a perfume factory. He'd come into the tent without them noticing, sidled up to Reynard and then put down his bag. He'd a white disposal overall in his hand and once he was clothed in it he got straight down to turning her over and commencing his superficial examination. The minute he got a good look at her he gasped.

'You alright Mossy?' asked Reynard.

'Yeah … it's just ... well I've a girl this age and … silly I know but … just for a moment. Anyway ...' his voice trailed away as he took a small hand recorder from his bag and began to dictate his observations into it.

Sergeant Hawkins in the meantime continued to remove the last bits of snow while Reynard, his eyes half closed to aid his concentration, was trying to imagine the girl's last moments and wondering why such an attractive young person had had her life so prematurely ended.

After a few minutes he shifted his position, edging round the two squatting men in order to see her better. She looked serene lying there so still; it was almost as if she were asleep. Her face was that of an English girl and she was unadorned by make-up apart from her lips which were red like her dress, and the dusting she had round her eyes which was brown. There was no sign of injury to her face but her throat was bruised, indicating she might have been strangled.

'Something here.' said the doctor, gently feeling a lump over one of her ears which was covered by hair and matted together with what would probably turn out to be blood. 'She's taken a knock here alright - a hefty one too.'

'A fatal blow?' asked Reynard.

'Could be.'

'How old d'you think she is? Geordie thinks she's mid to late thirties.'

'Yes … she's around that.'

The low cut velvet party dress she was wearing had a tight fitting bodice and a wide skirt, and it was the same bright colour as the shoe which had originally attracted Ringo's attention.

'Only the one shoe?' asked Reynard.

'So far; and a knitted hat to match.' Hawkins replied, standing again, his initial work done. Moss got up as well; he'd seen and recorded all he needed. The three men stood in silence gazing at the sorry scene. Hardened to violent and sudden death they still had the capacity to be horrified when the victim was someone who'd been so clearly full of life as this girl seemed to have been.

'Shocking waste.' said Geordie. 'A lovely lass and robbed of her life by some rotten bastard.'

Doctor Moss, even more used to cadavers than the other two and still struggling to keep his emotions in check, clamped his lips together and nodded.

Reynard shook his head. 'I don't know if I could cope with something like this if she were mine.'

'Me neither.' said Hawkins.

'You'd discount strangling then?' asked Reynard.

Moss rocked his head from side to side and sucked in a deep breath. 'Not entirely, not until I've investigated the head wound more thoroughly.'

'And what about … the 'er possibility of …?'

'Some form of sexual molestation? No I don't think so; there's nothing obvious of that nature. But that doesn't mean there hadn't been an intention to rape which led to the head wound. Incidentally I saw the ambulance arriving as I left the car park so if you've no further need of her here I'll take her after Geordie's finished; it's too cold and too depressing to stay here any longer than I have to.'

'I'd better check her pockets before she's moved.' said Reynard, bending to do so, only to find them empty apart from a blue ski mitten similar to the one they'd already found in the car park, a handkerchief, and a cloakroom ticket. 'That's odd.' he said slipping them into a plastic sachet; 'there's no purse, no loose coins, and no mobile … very strange. Make sure nothing drops out of her clothes when you move her boys otherwise I'm done.'

'Nothing'll be missed, Foxy, don't worry.'

'I'm going to slip down to the car park for a few minutes but I'll be back; there's often a few swivel-heads climb out of the woodwork when they hear an ambulance and it's not beyond the bounds of possibility one who knows something will today. If they do, and they're hanging around the car park to see what we're up to, I want to talk to them.

'Fair enough, but you're coming back here, aren't you … I mean …?'

'Of course, I want to see what's left on the sieve after you've put the snow through it.'

The spectators he'd hoped to find in the car park, drawn by the presence of the ambulance or their own guilty curiosity, never materialised. Not a soul showed up and before ten minutes had elapsed he was back with Geordie Hawkins and watching him finish the sieving. Almost immediately he spotted something on the wire mesh - a button. He bent and turned it over with a pencil he snatched from Hawkin's top pocket; it was stamped with the maker's name and was one of the type sewn onto working clothes or overalls by the manufacturer. This one was brown and it had gold lettering on it saying 'DENT'.

'Don't touch it.' screamed Reynard as Hawkins reached to pick it up. 'We might get a print.'

'Jesus, mate, you frightened the daylights out of me. I was only going to point to it.'

'Sorry Geordie,' said Reynard, 'I couldn't stop myself … it's the only thing we've got so far which looks half way useful. Check it when you get back to the lab, then let me have it back. It might have come off his clothes … it's hardly come from hers. Are you sure it was in the stuff which was covering her?'

'Absolutely dead certain, you can rely on it. I sieved the last bit myself and there it was.'

Reynard nodded.

'What d'you make of her, then?' Hawkins asked, 'And what d'you think might have happened?'

'Guess?'

'Yeah, sure, it's all we can do at this stage isn't it?'

'Take the dress first then, and the shoe. She's all dressed up, isn't she? I reckon she was going to a 'do', or at a 'do', or on her way home from one.'

'And?'

'And, look at the colour of her skin. She didn't get that tan from round here unless she's been sitting under a sun lamp.'

'She could be foreign.'

'True, but … oh I don't know - she looks English to me, local possibly, and she might have simply had a recent holiday abroad … she could even be getting coloured up ready to go on one, you know … a false tan.'

'My wife did the same last year before we went to Majorca,' said Hawkins 'bloody daft - I nearly did my flippin' nut. Twenty quid a throw she paid and it and it'd worn off before we got back.'

'Ah yes but by then the real thing had taken its place, hadn't it?'

'No it damned well hadn't we never saw the sun; it was cloudy the whole time.

Reynard, not wanting to be diverted by such a petty issue waved his hand dismissively. 'Yeah, yeah, bad luck, but let's get back to the girl. What do you make of the faint white mark on her finger?'

'Eh?'

'The white mark on her finger Geordie, you can see where she's been wearing a ring.' he said, pointing to it.

Geordie bent forward to get a closer look. 'Maybe she's divorced; she's a bit on the young side to be a widow … could have been an engagement ring.'

'Yeah … and maybe she'd lost it or left it in for repair. She could even have left it off because wanted to disguise the fact she was in a relationship. Suppose she was scheming to …'

'To 'play away' … you could be right; a ring on her finger would be a real 'put off' to any man.'

'True, but we're just guessing aren't we - better get on with what we know and leave the speculation until later - until after we've found out who she is. Our first priority has to be to get her positively identified, only then can we get stuck into everything else and find out what happened.'

Before Hawkins had time to answer him the sound of The William Tell Overture rang out. 'Bloody 'phone! Reynard' exclaimed, fishing his mobile from his jacket pocket and putting it to his ear.'

'Foxy?'

'Yes who's this?

'It's Charlie Hatton, John's Street. We've just had a 'phone call …'

'Charlie … I'm busy … what do you want?'

'Your office gave me your number. I've some information which might be of interest to you. A young woman was in here about half an hour ago reporting a possible 'Miss Per' and when I rang CID to give them the 'info' they told me you had a woman's body you haven't yet identified and I couldn't help …'

'Wondering if …'

'If my 'Miss Per' is your victim, yes.'

'I hope she is … if you know what I mean … I'll be on my way back to my office shortly and I'll call in on the way past. Any chance I can speak to …'

'Not a problem, 'Foxy' I'm on the front desk - I'll sort it when you come in.'

Hardly had Reynard finished struggling to put his mobile back into his jacket pocket than it started ringing again. Red in the face by then, he yanked up his overcoat and took it out. 'Yes?' he said, when he saw who was calling, 'Where are you?'

'I'm in the car park, Guv.' Groves answered. 'D.C. Best's with me. I'm just checking to make sure you were still up there before we walked up. We've a bit of news about the snow … and a horse box.'

'Stay where you are, they'll be taking the body soon; once it's gone I'll be on my way down. We have to go to John's Street and I think we should have a spell in the office to plan our next move after that. With luck we'll soon know who she is and … '

'Can we call into the University on the way?'

'… once we have her identified, we can start thinking of next of kin and then start … What's the university got to do with it?'

'They're only a mile away and they have security people on duty all night. If we contact whoever was on last night we can find out when it snowed.'

'OK.' he said, going back into the tent and asking Geordie if he'd finished.

Geordie nodded, and began packing up his things 'Yeah, all done. I've told the ambulance boys they can take her. Are you leaving someone here?'

'John's Street have a couple of lads on the way, the call I took was from Sergeant Hatton. He also told me …'

'Charlie Hatton?'

'Yeah, he reckons he knows who she is. If he's right … we're motoring.' said Reynard, 'Now don't forget to ring me as soon as you've checked the button for prints, and if you see the doc ask him how he's getting on with his preliminary report. I particularly want to know if the examination confirms his initial view there was no rape or sexual molestation. I know time of death is likely to be a problem, he's already intimated as much, so I presume everything's going to have to be gauged from circumstantial evidence.'

'You're probably right considering the recent low temperatures.' said Hawkins, collecting his things together.

'You wouldn't hang on for ten minutes until the coppers from John's Street arrive would you Geordie? I've got to go … the others are waiting for me.'

'I can't stay here long … you're not the only one who's busy you know.'

'Yes but …'

'Alright. Twenty minutes … and if no one's arrived by then I'm off. I'll see you sometime tomorrow.'

When Reynard got back to the car park he found Groves and Best squatting down examining the snow at the top end. 'Found anything?' he yelled.

'Plenty, and we're still trying to figure out how it all fits together. The tyre marks at the entrance seem to lead to and from two locations at opposite ends of the parking area. Question is ... how many vehicles were involved in making them? We've come to the conclusion there weren't many other than the Burgess's and our own, maybe only one or two, one of which came in and out of the car park more than once.'

'Sounds like progress. What can you tell about a vehicle from its tracks … its size I suppose?'

'More. We were talking to a local man about the different times the snow started and finished last night, and at the end the conversation he mentioned he'd seen a big darkish 4x4 backing a horse box trailer into the top corner, well out of sight of the road. It was around eight, when he was on his way to the Three Pigeons. The horse box was still there at ten thirty when he walked home again, but the vehicle he'd seen backing it in had gone. This morning when he left to drive his daughter to the station at seven, the car park was completely empty.'

'The horse box trailer had gone as well?'

'It had. Unfortunately the sun's thawing everything and the tracks are beginning to melt together. We won't get much more from them.'

'Is this location often used to leave trailers overnight?'

'He says it isn't, not on a regular basis anyway, and he ought to know because he lives in one of the cottages almost opposite.' said Best.

'And … what about on an irregular basis?'

'Yeah, it happens sometimes apparently, when a local household has a visitor with a big vehicle.'

'Like a caravan or a trailer?'

'Exactly.' Best replied, 'Looks like some local family had such a guest staying overnight. However it could also be that someone had a body to transport.'

'Risky … how big's this trailer … from its tracks?'

'Big enough for two horses, probably a four wheeler with two sets of wheels close together in the middle of the chassis.'

'And this man definitely saw no other vehicle?'

'He says he didn't.'

'OK.' said Reynard, 'So … to re-cap … it's looks as though a vehicle, a big dark coloured 4x4 probably, backed a horse box trailer into the car park sometime after seven last evening then uncoupled the trailer and drove off, returning at some time during the night or very early this morning to pick it up. And what about the other tracks you found; those made by the Burgess's car for example?'

'And our own, Guv. Both were easy to identify and to follow back to the entrance. However there was also another set of tyre marks which D.C Best and I think might be significant.'

'Aha. Did they belong to a big vehicle or a small one?'

'Hard to tell … biggish probably … but not as big as the one with the horse box, and with a different tyre pattern of which, I'm pleased to say, we got a good photograph.'

'Excellent, so you reckon you can distinguish one vehicle from another by its tyre pattern. Can you see enough detail to do that convincingly?'

'We think we can, but the tracks of all the vehicles except the horse box trailer which the sun can't reach are thawing fast so we have a few reservations on that score. However, and this is the good bit, if we're right the second vehicle never went anywhere near the horse box. *It* was only ever at the end of the car park where we and the Burgesses parked. We both drove across its tracks when we came in.'

'Right, so we've a lot to think about.'

'We sure do, and we're beginning to think this second vehicle might have been the one which squashed the ski mitten into the snow; its tyre tracks were just where the mitten was found.'

'Crikey, look at the time; we'd better get on.' said Reynard, 'We can talk as we go … first stop John's Street nick. You drive Constable.'

'What about the university, Guv?'

'You can have ten minutes there on the way. I assume you're trying to fix the time the tracks were made so you can work out when the victim got, or was brought to, the park?'

'Absolutely Guv, and then we have to tie it to the time of death.'

'Which the doctor hasn't given us yet. OK, we're finished here let's go back to the office and start to build the picture.'

Brighton Police Station
John's Street, Brighton Sussex
Monday 15th February 2010. 12.30. p.m.

Hey, Foxy,' said Sergeant Hatton, turning from the man he'd been talking to as they walked in. 'D'you want me to get you the W.P.C. who interviewed the young woman who came to report her friend missing?'

'Is she around?'

'That girl up in the park was murdered wasn't she?'

'Possibly.'

Hatton winked. 'You're not the only detectives you know - we know everything here - red dress wasn't it? Party girl?'

'I hope you don't mean what I think you mean. We've no idea who the victim is yet, let alone where she was going or from where she'd come.'

Hatton dropped the familiar approach he'd started with when he saw no response from Reynard, and spoke as he would have to any other senior officer. 'Go into the waiting room Sir, I'll find the W.P.C. and send her in.'

They were hardly seated when a young policewoman arrived, the Daily Report Book from the front desk in her hand.

Reynard smiled and introduced himself. He was about to introduce the other two as well when he realised Best wasn't with them. 'Where's he gone?' he asked Groves.

'He said he'll be here in a minute.'

'What's he …'

'He just wanted to say 'Hello' to the man who was talking to Sergeant Hatton when we arrived.'

'He just wanted to say 'Hello'! What's he think this is a dating agency … it's a murder investigation. Oh never mind lets' get started.'

As Reynard turned to the W.P.C., Best appeared, 'Sorry Guv that guy who was talking to Sergeant Hatton's a …'

'I don't give a damn what he is Constable, we haven't time to stand around chatting we've a killer to catch. Now can we start please?'

Best, looking aggrieved, took a seat and nodded to the W.P.C. opposite him as Reynard got the meeting under way.

'So what have you got for us Constable … er?'

'Carville Sir … Jane Carville. I've the notes of a conversation I had with a woman who called at ... let's see … yes here we are … it was at just after eleven this morning.'

'Her name?'

'Marion Palfrey, she's about twenty two and she reported a colleague of hers from work, a Roz Sommerton, seemed to have been missing since some time yesterday evening.'

'Some time yesterday evening … she couldn't be more specific?' asked Best, determined to show Reynard how committed he was.

'Give her a chance,' said Reynard, smiling inwardly when he saw what Best was up to. 'Go on Constable, what did this young woman have to say?'

'She said they were supposed to meet at Roz's place, a ground floor flat in one of the houses on Jutland Street. She was to be there at seven last night. They work for the local newspaper and were planning to attend an art exhibition of some sort at The Phoenix Gallery on which they were going to report. But when she got to the flat Roz wasn't there. She waited for half an hour outside but it started to snow and she got so cold she left and went home, assuming at any minute Roz would telephone to explain her absence and suggest meeting at the exhibition.'

'And did she?' asked Reynard.

'Phone? No … nor did she go to the exhibition, though Miss Palfrey did … on her own. And she didn't turn up for work this morning either, nor did she answer the messages Marion left on her land line or text messages on her mobile. In fact there was no contact at all, and she still wasn't at home when Marion went round again at ten to see if she was there.'

'Did you get a description of the missing woman?' asked Best.

'Oh yes … Roz Sommerton's around thirty five years of age, a slightly built woman of about five foot five or six, shoulder length light brown hair, and always smartly dressed … which for her generally means trousers rather than skirts. She's very much into suede boots at the moment and they're knee length as a rule, with her trousers tucked in the top. In view of the cold snap Marion thinks Roz may have been wearing long woollen dark blue coat and a scarlet beanie.'

'A what?' asked Reynard.

Groves laughed 'A beanie Sir. It's a sort of knitted pull-on skull cap.'

'Why didn't you say so then?' said Reynard, 'she was hardly wearing a vegetable.'

Best spluttered. 'You're thinking of a Scarlet Runner Guv, that's a bean.'

'No I wasn't, I was making sure you were awake.' retorted Reynard, 'I know damned well what a Scarlet Runner is, I grow them in my garden.'

'Yeah sorry, but the rest of the description sounds right for our victim though doesn't it?' said Best, keen to get back in favour. 'I mean her build, her hair, and her height, taken together with the coat and the hat seems about right doesn't it?

'Are you with us Sergeant.' said Reynard, turning to Groves. 'You haven't said much.'

'I've been thinking.'

'And are you going to share your thoughts? Are we to have the benefit of your opinion on the girl's clothing and general appearance, bearing in mind our victim wasn't in trousers?'

'Groves pursed her lips, raised her eyebrows, and slowly shook her head from side to side. 'Apart from asking if Miss Palfrey had mentioned ski mittens you are not Guv because … with a bit of luck … I'm going to jump ahead and show you a picture of Roz Sommerton, which I'm sure will soon solve the question of identity.'

'Are you indeed? How're you going to do that?'

Groves winked at Carville. 'Do I see a copy of this week's Globe on the side table?'

'You do,' Carville replied, reaching for it. 'it's the complimentary one all the stations get. D'you want it?'

'Please.' answered Groves, taking the paper from the W.P.C., opening it to page six and then pointing.

'Of course.' said Reynard, 'My wife reads her every week.'

'As do I.' Groves replied, laying the paper on the table and pointing to the inset thumbnail photograph of Roz

Sommerton at the top of her weekly column. 'Question is … is this the person we saw lying up there in the snow?'

Reynard and Best leaned over the tiny picture to get a better look. 'Could be;' said Best, 'but it's hard to be sure, her hair was all plastered down on her head when we saw her and her face was … well … expressionless. What d'you think Sir?'

Reynard slapped his knees, always a good sign as opposed to when he rubbed them, which was not. 'It looks like her alright … no dammit it is her … tell you what Constable …' he said, tapping Best's shoulder, 'drive round to The Globe's sub-office on the Old Worthing Road and see if you can pick up a couple of decent sized photographs of her; they'll soon confirm what we suspect. And, while you're doing it, Sergeant Groves and I can start putting a plan together. Alright? Let's get on with it then. Oh yes, and thank you Constable Carville you've been very helpful. Is there any chance you can scan the whole of your entry in the Daily Report Book and then e-mail it to me?'

'It'll be done within the next ten minutes Chief Inspector.' said Carville, as they all got up to go. 'Oh by the way,' she continued, 'I nearly forgot … you're to ring your office. They've message for you.'

'Really? Why … Oh I know, it'll be my 'phone again won't it.' he replied, fishing the instrument from his pocket. 'Thought so, switched off … damnation. Hang on a minute I'll see what they want.'

Carville left as Groves and Best resumed their seats and the Inspector punched in his office number.

'D.C.I. Reynard,' he said when his call was answered, 'have you a message for me?'

The answer was obviously 'Yes', and he listened without interrupting for several minutes before closing his 'phone. 'Right, we're off.' he said, 'Change of plan; I'll fill you in on the way. You can drop Sergeant Groves and I back at the office Constable then you can go to the Globe's office and pick the photographs, they'll have plenty.'

'Suppose I go with him?' said Groves, 'I could have another chat with Marion Palfrey and take a quick look around Roz's desk and her locker, if she has one?'

'No, you stay with me. As soon as we get back to Sussex House I want you to get in your car and drive to Dorchester where they've a purse I want to examine. That's what the telephone call was about. And you'll have to go and have a chat with this man while you're down there.' he said, passing her a note he'd written during the 'phone call. 'He's the chap who owns the horse box we're interested in … and he's just handed in a purse. It's all on this piece of paper.'

'Is our luck changing … sounds like it?

'Read the note. 'Mr Bow …' something.'

'Bowtell … And will you want me back at the office tonight, or will tomorrow morning do?'

'Ring me before you leave Dorchester in case I think of something else,' said Reynard, 'otherwise we'll all meet in my office tomorrow … good and early mind. Come on, let's get on with it.'

They got up and were about to leave when Best stopped. 'Did we get Roz Sommerton's address?'

'It'll be in the e-mail the constable's sending me when she's scanned the page in the report book, why?' asked Reynard 'We still don't know for sure whether the woman who's missing is our victim.'

'I think the report said Jutland Street,' said Groves, 'Number Three.

Reynard smiled at her and turned to Constable Best. 'Don't go chasing round there until we know for sure whether the Miss Per this station's investigating, and the woman the dog found up at Fyling Castle, is one and the same person.'

'I wasn't thinking of going round.' said Best, not yet anyway. I was thinking about what I was told a couple of minutes before I came into this room by the man who was talking to Sergeant Hatton when we came in. He was on the Advanced Driver's course with me; his name's Furness, he's a D.C attached to Shoreham nick, and he mentioned he was on his way to interview a man who lives in Armada Street about a serious crime.'

'Yes? So what? asked Reynard.

'It's a little street which runs down one side of The Feathers Hotel; Jutland Street runs down the other; between them they divide the terrace into three.'

'Roz Sommerton lives in Jutland Street.' exclaimed Groves

'What's this 'serious crime' your friend's investigating?' Reynard asked.

'Attempted rape.'

Reynard's eyebrows shot up so far they met his curly hair. 'Stone the crows.'

'I couldn't have put it better, Guv,' said Groves. 'what a turn up.'

'If it's rape *we* ought to be looking at him as well.' said Reynard. 'Nip out and see if your pal's gone. We'll wait here.'

Carville shook her head. 'You're too late, he *has* gone; I saw him drive off through the window.'

'So it's back to Plan One, OK?'

'Plan One, what's that?' asked Best

'It's you dropping me at Sussex House and then going on to pick the photos from The Globe … while Sergeant Groves makes for Dorchester. Right? Got it? Any questions?'

'No, Guv.' they echoed.

'OK off we go … and thank you.' said Reynard to W.P.C. Carville as they rose from their seats, 'I'll get back to you if I need anything else but call me immediately if Marion Palfrey contacts you again.'

Sussex Police Major Incident Suite, Sussex House, Brighton Sussex. Monday 15th February 2010. 1.34. p.m.

Best had driven off, and Groves was racing up to the office to collect her laptop prior to leaving for Dorchester when Reynard was stopped by the desk Sergeant, a long-time friend of his. 'You've investigating the Sommerton case aren't you, Foxy?'

'I might be,' Reynard answered cautiously, 'why d'you want to know?'

'I've left an e-mail on your desk; Dorchester sent it an hour ago. It was addressed to 'Officer in charge of the Rosaleen Sommerton case.' They obviously didn't know who that was. Nor did I, but Jack Crowther told me you had it.'

'Yes. I was on to someone there about twenty minutes ago and they told me they'd sent it. What else did they say?'

'It seems some local guy found a woman's handbag or purse in the back of his horse box this morning. He handed it in when he opened it and found it was stuffed with Credit and Press cards in the name of Rosaleen Sommerton. There was no money so he thought some kids might have found it or stolen it, pocketed the cash, and chucked the purse in the back of his trailer. Someone in Dorchester rang the Head Office of The Globe when they spotted where she worked, but *it's* in Horsham and she works out of a sub office in Brighton. When they rang there they got no answer. I wrote it all down; it's on your desk'

'Fair enough. As a matter of fact I decided to send Sergeant Groves down there after I'd taken the call.' Reynard replied, heading for the stairs and almost colliding with Groves at the top, as she came flying round the corner with her lap top in her hand.

'Blimey, where's the fire?'

Groves laughed. 'I want to get back before seven, I'm going out.'

'Ooh … anywhere nice?'

'Guv, it's just to the cinema with my sister, but we're meeting outside at eight.'

'We've time for some coffee before you go; and there's an e-mail on my desk which we should see before you leave.'

'Fair enough, but I must be on my way by two.'

Once in his office Reynard set about pulling mugs out of his desk drawer and filling them with coffee. Groves watched with a condescending smile then slowly shook her head as she returned to her thoughts on the case. 'She never saw it coming, did she, Guv? She was expecting a quiet evening in a gallery with free drinks and a nibble or two thrown in, and instead she wound up being murdered and shoved into a snow drift.'

'I know,' said Reynard, rubbing his chin with one hand and stirring sugar into his coffee with the other. 'and it's up to us to find out why it all went so badly wrong - what drove someone to kill her. Maybe the e-mail will give us a clue.'

He picked up the printout of the scanned notes the constable in Dorchester had taken and read it twice before passing it over to Groves.

Information given by Leslie Bowtell, owner of Foxhunter Riding School, West Overton, Wiltshire.

Mr Bowtell stayed overnight in his sister's house, Green Gables, Falmer's Hill, Brighton, last night - 14th/15th February having picked up a horse box he'd just bought on e-Bay from Norman Townley, of Blackmeade Farm, Saddlecombe Basset, Sussex.

The completely empty two horse box had been padlocked and left overnight in car park at Fyling Castle, across the road from his sister's house which had a gateway too narrow to take it.

Early this morning at around six am he went to the car park, unlocked the box, hitched it up, and drove it home.

On arriving in his yard he was checking his new purchase when he spotted a red silk purse lying on the floor. It hadn't been there the day before. He opened it and seeing the contents assumed it to have been stolen. He brought it into Dorchester Police Station on his way to a local feed merchant's at 12.15 p.m.

Please advise address to which purse should be sent.

W.P.C. Avril Nash, Dorchester Police Station 15.30. p.m. 15th February, 2010.

'Looks like we're losing a suspect Lucy. This man isn't our killer, but the purse is a bit of luck, it'll help confirm who our victim is.'

'Roz Sommerton?'

Reynard nodded. 'You'd better collect the purse before you go to see Mr Bowtell, and don't forget to telephone me here before you leave Dorchester.'

'Want me to …?'

Before she could finish the sentence D.C. Best walked in. 'Ah coffee … any for me?'

'Depends what you've got.' said Reynard.

'Very little I'm afraid; there was no one in the Globe's office and everything was locked up. I went into the Pharmacy and asked the girl at the counter if she'd seen anyone going up to it but she hadn't.'

'There's another mug in the cupboard behind you … help yourself.' said Reynard. 'Now … go on Sergeant, you were about to say something before you left.'

'Well I was going to ask if you wanted me to go to Roz Sommerton's flat now … I can manage half an hour before I go to Dorchester … see if I can get in … have a chat with the neighbours and so on.'

Reynard looked at his watch. 'Hmm … Two and half hours to Dorchester, an hour there and two and half back … you'll not be in Brighton again much before eight … tight. But if you can manage twenty minutes to stop by at Roz Sommerton's flat on the way and have a quick look for her mother's address I'd be grateful; I want to let her know what's happened. The flat's the most likely place to find it and I'd go myself, but I must have a chat with Doctor Moss first. You go with her Constable, and wait there for me; I'll be with you as soon as I can. Our first priority is to get hold of this girl's next of kin - her mother in other words - and once we have it we can break the news. Best and I can do that while you're in Dorchester Sergeant; the purse is a priority too. Right? Everyone clear as to what they have to do? Good, I'm off to see Doctor Moss; I only hope he's sobered up after all the whisky I saw him knocking back. O.K. let's go. We'll meet up here again tomorrow morning at eight.'

Brighton and District Mortuary,
Lewes Road, Brighton.
Monday 15th February 2010. 2.45. p.m.

Doctor Moss saw Reynard walking into the building from his window and went down to the reception desk to meet him. Reynard could smell the whisky when he was still ten feet away.

'Got anything for me?' Reynard asked.

'I haven't even started and I'm not sure I will this afternoon.'

'Why what's wrong. This is urgent.'

'I know it is Foxy but, as I told you this morning, I've a cold coming on and I'm not sure I'm up to it … not today anyway. I'd give it to my deputy Doctor Vladic but he's already up to his neck with …'

'No I want you to do this one yourself Mossy - the time of death's going to be tricky - you said so yourself - and Vladic's barely out of college, he hasn't half the experience you've got.'

'He'll do a good job. Trouble is he's already stuck into a tricky one brought in during the night; he'll be the rest of the day on it. I've cleaned our lady up a bit though … got her undressed and so on. If you like to come through we can have a quick look at her. Here,' he said, stifling a sneeze as he handed Reynard an overall and a cap, 'stick these on; you know the rules.'

'Rules … rules … we're strangled with bloody rules Mossy.' Reynard replied, cladding himself as they walked into the post mortem room.

Doctor Moss's assistant Doctor Vladic was standing beside a man's body which was on a stainless steel bench; he was making a very large incision in the corpse's abdomen. A junior assistant who looked no more than a schoolboy was wheeling a trolley into position under a battery of overhead lamps. On it and covered by a sheet, was a figure which looked as though it might be that of a woman. 'Is this one mine?' asked Reynard

'I think so … let's have a look.' answered Moss.

The assistant, seemingly happy with the trolley's position, went over to talk to Doctor Vladic who was groping about inside the cavity he'd opened up, leaving Moss and Reynard looking at the remains of Rosaleen Sommerton.

'Bloody waste.' Reynard mumbled as Moss pulled back the sheet to reveal the head and the upper body of the woman they'd last seen lying face down in the snow. 'Still no sign of molestation when you removed her clothes then, nothing torn or looking as though it might have come as a result of her resisting a sexual attack of any sort?'

'Only her finger nails: two on one hand were broken, and some fibrous residue which might tell us something was under an unbroken one on the other.'

'Nothing which could yield DNA?'

'Not really.'

'No defensive wounds or anything of that nature?'

'Not at first sight. And there's no sign to say she suffered much either, other than the bruise marks on her throat we saw when we were up in the park and a few on her upper arms we've just seen. More significant is the lump on the side of her head I mentioned up in the tent.'

'And d'you reckon that's what killed her?'

'It certainly could have. Just above your ear's a very vulnerable place.'

'And it's all you've found so far is it, there were no other detectable wounds?'

'No, just the blow to her temple and the bruising on her arms and throat. Here … look for yourself.' said Moss, pulling the sheet fully back.

'And rape's out?'

'I think so, though intercourse may not be. I'll tell you tomorrow. If I'm not in, Vladic'll 'phone you.'

'OK Mossy.' said Reynard, bending down and examining every bit of the woman's corpse he could see without touching her, and paying particular attention to her arms, her hands, and her fingers. After a minute or two he straightened up, he'd seen nothing to indicate how she'd died other than the marks which had already been discussed. 'What about elsewhere under her hair?' he asked.

'Nothing other than the swelling we've just discussed; I'll be looking at her in more detail later. Seen enough?'

'Too much. You'll let me have the result of the internal examination won't you, Mossy … and your best shot at the time of death. Ring me.'

'Yeah … tomorrow afternoon … if I'm in.'

'Oh God I hope you are; I'm relying on you.'

'One thing before you go … I don't know whether you noticed anything significant about the disposition of the bruise marks on her arms?'

'The finger marks yes, what about them?'

'She was held from behind. There could have been two people of course - one who held her by her arms, and one who hit her on the head.'

'Two killers? Crikey, on that depressing note I'll leave you. Contact me as soon as you have anything concrete on the time of death.'

'I will; and if I don't Doctor Vladic will.'

'Go home and fill yourself up with your damned hot whisky then Mossy, and make sure you're in tomorrow. Don't let me down.'

'Have I ever?'

'I won't answer that you crafty old sod, because you'll twist whatever I say and make me feel guilty when I'm not.' Reynard replied, stripping off his overalls and heading for the door.

3A Jutland Street, Brighton.
Monday 15th February 2010. 2.50 p.m.

Sergeant Groves and Constable Best stood at the front door of Roz Sommerton's flat once the basement entrance to the house. It was dark, even so early in the afternoon, being set back and tucked beneath steps leading up to the cleverly constructed side by side doors of apartments 3B and 3C, which looked as though they'd always been there and not put in to replace the original single one when the house had been converted into flats.

Her knock had produced no response and Groves was about to try looking through one of the two front windows when her attention was caught by a plant pot lying on its side; its frostbitten geranium broken off at the base of the stem. When she righted it she saw the key; a newly cut one without ring or fob. Whether it had been hidden under the pot or dropped to the ground and then accidentally covered when it was tipped over wasn't obvious. In a way it was surprising she'd seen it at all; there was no street lamp to illuminate the darkness where she stood. *Had* Roz Sommerton dropped it without realizing she'd done so? Or had someone else let it fall or knocked it from her hand and not noticed?

Groves hammered on the door then, opening the letter box shouted at the top of her voice. 'Ms Sommerton are you there; it's the police, I'm Sergeant Groves, let me in please.'

'She might have dropped it without knowing.' said Best. 'it mightn't even be for this flat.'

'Only one way to find out.' replied Groves, inserting the key into the lock. 'But let's make absolutely sure there's no one at home first … her mother maybe … we don't want to be caught 'breaking and entering'.'

Best nodded and hammered on the door with his fist. When there was no response he opened the letter box and shouted: 'Anyone there … are you alright … it's the police … Sergeant Groves and Constable Best … would you let us in please.'

There was no response.

Groves went to the window. The curtains were drawn but she could tell there was no light on inside. Not that she expected there to be one for Best's knock had echoed hollowly as though the flat was unoccupied.

She turned the key, pushed the door open and, continuing to call out as she went, entered the flat; her torch in her hand. Just inside the door was a light switch. She turned it on and discovered she was in long narrow hallway. The right hand wall ran unbroken other than a few pegs on which some coats were hanging, until it came to a door facing her at the end. Next to it was a second door; both were shut. On her left and barely inside the flat at all, a third door stood slightly ajar. She pushed it fully open, switched on the light, and went in, followed by Best.

It was a large room - the full width of the house apart from the hall - and it clearly served as living room and kitchen. It was so neat and tidy it gave the impression of not being lived in at all. When they looked around more carefully though they saw there were a few things on the draining board to contradict such an assumption … a mug, a plate, and a few pieces of cutlery were standing in a draining basket on the edge of the sink; clearly they'd been in recent use. In the middle of the dining room table was a bud vase containing a single rose; propped against it was a birthday card, and beside it an envelope. Best picked the card up; it had a picture of a Cocker Spaniel puppy on the front and a short message written inside: 'Happy Birthday, Mum, I'll try to get to see you next weekend. All my love … Rosaleen.'

Groves pointed to the envelope; it was stamped, and addressed to Charlotte Sommerton, Rosemount, Frenchman's Lane, Upper Beeding, Sussex.

'You're in for a nasty shock by the look of things you poor soul.' Groves muttered, as she pulled one of the dining room chairs from under the table, swung it round to face the room, and sat on it.'

'So what d'you think?' she asked Best, 'No personal touches in evidence at all except for this card for her mother. It's not a bad place though … comfortable ... expensively furnished … no shortage of money obviously.'

'I agree … you should see where I live.' said Best.

Groves smiled 'Am I to take that as an invitation?'

'If you like … but no, joking apart, this is a damned nice flat even if it does look more like a show house than a home. Look at how precisely she's placed the furniture. Look at how evenly apart the pictures are. And there're no books, newspapers, magazines, nothing at all lying about on the furniture or the floor.'

'Whereas in your place …?'

'Shut up Sarge. All I'm saying is the flat tells us nothing about Roz Sommerton except she's tidy and has good taste.'

Groves clapped her hands together and stood up. 'Dead right.' she said. 'What next?'

'We could check the desk if you like, or would you rather we had a quick look round rest of the place.'

'Have a look round I think.' replied Groves.

The bathroom, which lay behind the door facing them as they walked down the corridor, gave no clues either. Only the half empty strip of contraceptive pills, modestly hidden in the cabinet, told more of her than the usual selection of toiletries which were openly on view.

The bedroom, which they entered last, was different. Here there was evidence of hurried activity: wardrobe doors left open; clothes half pulled out of drawers and not pushed back in properly; several pairs of shoes and a pair of knee length tan coloured suede boots lying about the floor or under the dressing table; and two dresses and a jacket cast untidily on the bed with a some underwear a pair of dark trousers a white silk shirt and a pale blue pullover.

The dressing table was covered with a whole lot of fancy shaped bottles and jars. All had make-up in them. In the centre of the jumble of powder, perfume, lipstick, and eye shadow was her jewellery: a great tangle of funky necklaces and beads in an open casket, and a small red velvet lined jewellery box crammed full of rings and earrings.

Best seemed to be mesmerised by the muddle all round them. 'Blimey,' he said, 'it's a bit different to the living room … I'm not poking about in all this stuff.'

'Go back and have a shot at the desk then. I'll deal with this room and then I'm off. Oh, and would you ring the

Governor and tell him we've found the girl's mother's address, and that I'll be leaving in five minutes.'

Best nodded and went back to the sitting room, his mobile in his hand, leaving Groves looking at a long, African, primitive style wooden bead necklace. Each sphere on it was the size of a golf ball. 'Nice.' she said, holding it up to herself and looking in the mirror.

She tried the wardrobe next … and chest of drawers. They were full of clothes which were both expensive and elegant. Right at the back was another pair of knee length boots, black ones. Roz Sommerton had some fancy kit Groves concluded as she left the room to return to the living room.

'How are you getting on?' she asked Best, who was going through one of the desk's drawers.

'Not much in this one so far,' he replied, 'just a few bank statements, a load of correspondence about the flat, her passport, and her diary. The other one was full of things about her work … notes for articles, drafts of others, some pages of text implying she was writing a book. I found her diary on the top … it's chock full of aide-memoire notes, appointments, addresses, and 'phone numbers … I reckon we ought to take it all with us to check in the office … it'll take hours to go through it thoroughly. I also found this card cello-taped to a cellophane sleeve which must have had the rose in it; she'd screwed it up and chucked into the waste paper basket.'

'Any message on it?'

'Yeah, a rather brief one which simply says 'From Chef with love.''

'Chef? … I wonder who the hell he is … a boyfriend?'

'You mean her boyfriend's a chef?'

'Yes, possibly … unless it was short for something.'

'Like what?'

'Cheffington.'

'Chessington? No, that's a zoo.'

'No, Cheffington, two f's … Oh forget it, I'm just kidding. Maybe it isn't short for anything. It could even be a nickname or a joke name for someone who can't cook. Let's not get bogged down trying to puzzle it out; what else did you find of interest'

'Not much.'

'Well, we have the mother's address and that's what the governor wanted, so I'll be off. You could make a start on the diary if you like, while you wait for 'his nibs' to arrive.'

'Will do.' said Best, as Groves buttoned up her coat and made for the door.

She'd hardly gone when D.C.I Reynard turned up and rang the bell below the knocker.

Best put down the diary he'd been reading and let him in. 'Did you see the doc Sir,' he said, as they progressed into the living room.

'Reynard grunted, brushed his head with his hand to remove to the light dusting of snow from his hair and then took off his coat and draped it over the back of a chair. 'It's started to come down again.'

'So I see Sir. Heavy is it? Was the doc there?'

'He was at first he'd waited for me, but he was going home when I left, says his cold's getting worse. We'll have to work with his deputy Dr Vladic if he doesn't turn in tomorrow.' said Reynard, 'Bloody man, I knew this was going to happen when I saw all that whisky he was shifting.'

'He was coughing a lot.'

'Yeah … and drinking a lot! Filling himself up all morning and now he's gone home with a hangover he's trying to tell us is a cold. I knew it would happen it was sticking out a mile. So what have you found?'

'Not much … not yet anyway. Me and the Sarge had a look round all the rooms and then more or less as soon as we'd found the mother's address, she headed off for Dorchester. She's not long gone. She told me to make a start on the contents of the writing desk beginning with the diary. I was reading it when you knocked.'

'Right, you carry on with that while I have a poke round … familiarise myself with the place. I dare say we'll be in and out of here quite a few times before we're finished.'

'I doubt you'll find much other than what's in her desk, *it's* full of stuff alright, but we saw nothing of interest anywhere else. Strange woman though … tidy as hell in here and the bathroom but her bedroom's an absolute shambles - things all over the place.'

'Right.' said Reynard, going out into the hall again. 'I'll just have a shufti … see if I can spot anything you two missed. You stick with the diary.'

He looked back into the living room as he stood in the doorway.' What's that card on the table Constable?'

'It's a birthday card … one for her mother. It's all written up and addressed ready to go. That's how we found the address. She lives in Upper Beeding …'

'Oh yeah … lying on the table like this was it?'

'Yes.'

'She must have just got it ready to post.'

'That's what I thought … it only needed sticking down. I reckon she was going to post it when she went out last night but for some reason forget to pick it up.'

'Taken together with the mess you say I'll find in the bedroom it points to an unexpected and hurried departure. I wonder if it was an enforced one.'

'Yeah, I wonder.'

'She could have been abducted … or maybe she was just late and left in a rush. It'll be interesting trying to work out what prompted the rapid departure. OK. Let me have a quick snoop and then we'll go and inform her mother.

'And I found this,' said Best, handing Reynard the cellophane wrapping.'

'Aha! … Who d'you think Chef is?'

'A boyfriend perhaps.'

'Maybe … yes, maybe.' Reynard replied, heading for the bedroom.

Two minute later he was back.

'What did you make of the mess?' asked Best.

'I want to go back to the office now;' said Reynard, you can leave everything here except the diary … we'll be back again tomorrow more than likely.'

'But what did you make of the mess in the bedroom?'

'You're not married are you Norman?' Reynard replied, addressing him by his given name instead of 'Next', like everyone else. 'You've a lot to learn Constable … even the most meticulously tidy woman flings her stuff in every direction if she's in a panic over what to wear. Had she not been in such a big hurry she have picked everything up and put it away. No … something happened … or someone came to make her fly round, and it's up to us to find out what or who it was.'

***

Groves got to Dorchester after an easy run through the light afternoon traffic, picked up the purse from the Police Station in Weymouth Avenue and then drove over to West Overton to talk to Mr Bowtell.

He'd nothing much to add to what he'd said to W.P.C. Nash in Dorchester earlier - information she'd passed on to Reynard in the e-mail. He'd dropped the horse box off at around seven just as the man on his way to the pub had told them, and he'd done so for the reason which had already been suggested … the entrance gate of his sister's house where he was staying overnight was too narrow. At 6 a.m. he'd retrieved the horse box trailer and driven to his home at West Overton. It was only when he was showing his wife what he'd bought, he found the purse.

Once Groves saw there was little more to be got from him she left, stopping on the way back to grab a cup of coffee and a bite to eat, for she'd practically forgotten about food since breakfast time.

She tried to ring D.C.I. Reynard as she ate her snack meal to tell him what she'd discovered from Mr Bowtell and to find out how he'd got on at Roz Sommerton's. But she couldn't get through. 'He's turned the damned thing off again,' she said to herself. 'Anyway, they'll probably be at the mother's place by now giving her the bad news. I may as well go home.'

Rosemount, Frenchman's Lane, Upper Beeding, BN40 3 WF Monday 15th February 2010 8.46 pm.

It was snowing again by the time they got to Mrs Sommerton's bungalow at the top of the lane. The street light at her gate, the only one in sight as far as they could see, was giving a yellow glow to the snow surrounding the house and it reminded them of a Christmas card.

'No light on Sir.' said Best. 'Maybe she's out.'

'Maybe she is … go and give her a knock she might be in a back room. She could have gone to bed.'

'I wondered that, old folks often turn in early.'

'Yeah maybe … it's possible.' said Reynard, 'If Roz was thirty five or so her mother must be about what, sixty odd? She's not old, she'll still be up if she's there.'

'OK, I'll see if she's in then.' Best got out of the car and went up to the door.

As he passed the front room window he noted the curtains weren't drawn. When his knock failed to produce a response he pushed up the flap on the letter box and looked in. Light from the lamp at the gate filtering into the hall through a glass panel over the front door illuminated not only the hall but the room at the end of it - which looked as though it was the kitchen. They both had a curious air of abandonment about them. It was as though whoever lived there had gone away.

'Not a sausage Sir,' Best yelled to Reynard, who'd turned the car and was sitting watching him through the open window.

'Try her neighbour.' Reynard shouted back.

Best made one last attempt by banging on the door with his fist. Reynard didn't like it. 'For God's sake man you'll frighten the wits out of her try next door.'

'OK … on my way, Sir.'

Three minutes later he was back at the car. He got in before saying anything.

'What is it?' asked Reynard.

'You're not going to believe this Guv … she's dead; died a couple of days ago on Saturday night around ten. An ambulance was there half ten … the neighbour heard it arrive and got up to look out of his window. About fifteen minutes later they took her out on a stretcher and went tearing off.'

'Sounds fishy. Why didn't he go out when the ambulance was there? How did he know she was dead? Some neighbour.'

'A copper from Steyning came round Sunday morning checking the place was fully secured. *He* told him.'

'Hmm, what else did the neighbour say?'

'Not much. Mrs Sommerton kept herself to herself apparently. It suited him because he lives alone and prefers his own company too. It seems they had very little contact other than an occasional 'Good Morning' or 'Good Afternoon' when they saw each other in their gardens. The copper from Steyning who came round told him the ambulance was called by person who wouldn't give a name. It must have been someone who was with her when she died, I reckon, and didn't want to get involved.'

'Or whoever it was attacked her got a guilty conscience or panicked when they saw how badly they'd injured her and then called for the ambulance. Something funny going on here Constable: first the mother, then the daughter … they must be connected. Where d'you say that copper was from … Steyning?' Let's drive round and see what they can tell us.'

***

Groves was on the motorway heading back to Brighton by the time Reynard and Best got to Steyning Police Station.

'I'll do the talking,' said Reynard, 'we don't want to get bogged down in a debate.'

'I'll wait in the car if you'd rather Sir.' Best replied.

'No, it'll be better if we both hear what they have to say then we'll be sure we don't forget anything.'

As it happened they were only there twenty minutes because the first policemen they spoke to was the one the duty sergeant had sent out to Mrs Sommerton's when the ambulance crew telephoned in to report Mrs Sommerton's death.

'So what did you find when you got there?' asked Reynard, taking a notebook out of his pocket and handing it to Best, who nodded and fished a pencil from his own.

'I got there in about ten minutes.' the constable replied, 'They already had her on a stretcher and were putting her in the ambulance to take her to hospital when I arrived. One of the stretcher men told me she'd had a heart attack and died on her kitchen floor. I asked him who else was in the house. He said the door was open when they got there but there was no one around. He'd no idea who'd sent for them. I've since discovered the call was made from a box on the corner. Personally, I reckon …'

'Leave your reckoning for the moment please Constable - if you don't mind.' said Reynard. What do you actually know?'

The constable, somewhat in awe of the county's most famous detective and unsettled by the mild reprimand he'd been given, went silent. Clearly he hadn't enjoyed being pulled up and looked to Best for support, but Best knew when to keep quiet and say nothing.

'Come on man,' said Reynard, 'what did the caller say for Goodness's sake - his exact words if you can remember them?'

'Yes Sir, well apparently the caller told the ambulance station a woman had died of a heart attack and was lying on the floor of her kitchen and they …'

'*He* … are you sure it was a '*he*'?'

'Yes, it was definitely a man. He gave the address, told them the door was open, and rang off saying he didn't want to get involved.'

'Hmm. Pity. And was a doctor called?'

'Not as far as I know, but the one in the casualty department at the hospital certified the death when the body was bought in. He told me himself when I spoke to him yesterday.'

'Nothing suspicious?'

'He didn't say there was, and I didn't ask. I had no reason to because I'd looked round the house myself and saw no sign of anything which looked as though she'd had an accident or fallen or been pushed or anything like that; and there was no sign of a break-in or a struggle. The place looked just as you'd expect for a lady of her age living on her own - neat and tidy, and full of photographs.'

'Well put; so you locked up and left?'

'Yes Sir, locked up and went round to talk to her neighbours.'

'And…?'

'One wasn't there and still isn't, a widow who also lives alone. She's in Sardinia on holiday with her son and his family, been there a week, won't be back for another. The man on other side told me yesterday he didn't usually see much of Mrs Sommerton but knew she had a heart condition. They have the same doctor seemingly, so I rang him. When I told him what had happened he confirmed she'd a history of minor heart attacks, and he wasn't at all surprised to hear she appeared to have died of one.'

'Appeared?

'Yes, 'appeared'.'

'So she only *appeared* to have …'

'No, sorry Sir, it's just the way I put it; the doctor had no doubt Mrs Sommerton died of natural causes. Anyway the autopsy the coroner's ordered will confirm it one way or the other. It's being done in the hospital it might have been done already, I'll check if you like. Is that why you're here - you think there's something odd about her death?'

'Not really, we're investigating the murder of her daughter sometime late yesterday afternoon or early evening.'

'Crikey! … What a coincidence.'

'Really, a coincidence? I don't think so. Do you know what a coincidence is Constable: it's an *unlikely* situation waiting for a *likely* explanation. And that's our job isn't it - digging out likely explanations?'

The constable looked at him blank faced.

'Ah never mind. So the neighbour saw Mrs Sommerton going out on a stretcher. Who told him she was dead?'

'I did Sir, when I went round yesterday morning to ask him what he knew about her. He'd seen the ambulance taking her away and wanted to know what had happened.'

'What about her family, anyone told them?'

'There's just the one daughter - Rosaleen. Oh my God, it's her who's been murdered isn't it? No wonder I got no answer when I rang. I even drove down to Brighton yesterday afternoon in the hope of catching her but she wasn't in. My calls were unanswered again today. Now I know why.'

'Who's doing the autopsy?'

'Someone in the hospital.'

'Not our man, not Doctor Moss?'

'Doctor Moss, no. They gave me his name - foreign - unpronounceable …Val someone.'

'Ah yes … Doctor Vladic. Fair enough, you've been very helpful. Now … have you a key to Mrs Sommerton's house?'

'Yes, there's one here.'

'Can we borrow it?'

'I suppose so, I'll ask the sergeant. D'you reckon the old lady was murdered as well?'

Reynard shook his head. 'I've no idea, but for the moment we'll assume what you've told us is the case, that she died naturally of a heart attack. No, we're here because we want to see if we can find anything in her house to help us identify her daughter's killer. Now, can we have the key please?'

Twenty minutes later they were at Mrs Sommerton's bungalow again, and opening the door.

Half an hour after that they were on their way back to Steyning to return the key. The house had delivered nothing to help them, and they'd packed up for the day telling the duty sergeant at Steyning they'd probably be back again before long.

Tuesday 16th February

Sussex Police Major Incident Suite,
Sussex House, Brighton Sussex.
Tuesday 16th February 2010. 8.00 a.m.

Good morning.' said Detective Chief Inspector Reynard, shaking his head to throw off the snow which had gathered on it as he'd leaned into the blizzard sweeping through the car park, and then unbuttoning his coat.

'Morning Sir.' answered Best, who'd got in very early and was already seated with an open file of case papers across his knees.

D.S. Groves who'd only arrived seconds in front of the D.C.I. and was still shaking flakes off her coat, asked him if Superintendent Bradshaw had spoken to him.

'When?'

'Just now; I bumped into him in the corridor, he asked me if I'd seen you, it seemed urgent. I told him you'd just driven in.'

'I wonder who's been eating his porridge?' said Reynard, taking off his overcoat and giving it a good shake before hanging it on a hook it behind the door.

'Not a clue, Sir,' said Groves.

'And he stopped *me* on the stairs half an hour ago and asked if you were around.' added Best. 'I told him we had a meeting scheduled for eight and that you'd surely be in for it.'

'Oh … right … I'd better see what he wants. Give me a few minutes to check and then we'll exchange information about how we all got on yesterday.'

Groves took a seat and opened her brief case. 'Mind if we help ourselves to …'

'No, no, carry on, I won't be long.'

As soon as Reynard was out of the room and heading in the direction of Superintendent Bradshaw's office, Groves was up and out of her chair. 'With or without?' she asked Best, picking up the coffee jug from its heating mantle and a pint plastic bottle of full fat milk from the top of the filing cabinet.

'With.' said Best. 'Dare we risk taking a 'you know what'?'

'Oh no … I'm not going to be caught with my hand in his drawers' she said, immediately giggling at her unfortunate choice of words. 'But suit yourself, maybe you're braver than I am.'

'I doubt it Sarge, I'll wait.' Best said.

***

Chief Superintendent Colin Bradshaw swung round from his computer screen as soon as Reynard entered the office and waved him to a seat in front of the desk. 'I've got a present for you Foxy.'

'A present … oh good … what is it this time?

'A suspect; a man who may be connected …'

'To one of my cases?'

'If you wait a minute I'll tell you.'

'It's the murdered girl isn't it?'

'Wait wait wait … this isn't a guessing game. If you give me chance I'll fill you in. Yes it is about the murder … what's the girl's name again, Rosaleen something or other? Summers wasn't it?'

'Sommerton Sir, but she's known as Roz to everyone we've spoken to so we thought she'd better be Roz to us as well - it'll prevent confusion.'

'Well her anyway … Roz … yes … awful name I wonder why she changed it.'

'Too late to ask her now; who knows? Young people like racy names I suppose and Rosaleen's a bit old fashioned for a high flyer like this lass - well woman really - she looked well over thirty to me. It's an Irish name - my grandmother was called Rosaleen - she came from Cork.'

'Really … yes … well … OK we'll stick to Roz. I didn't bring you in to query her name though, it was something different. When I was glancing through yesterday's incident log I noticed Jack Crowther had been speaking to a D.C. from Shoreham about a man who lives in Armada Street. Isn't that the one next to Jutland Street where your victim lived?'

'If she turns out to be who we think she is - yes. Jutland and Armada Streets run parallel to each other down either side of The Feathers Hotel; it occupies the whole block between the two of them.'

'Ah yes, the hotel's the middle section of Trafalgar Terrace on the sea front, I know it. Well it seems this man's wanted for questioning regarding the attempted rape of a young female work colleague at Shoreham Power Station, and I couldn't help wondering if he might just be …'

'Ah, him. Yes, I know about him. One of my team knows the D.C. from Shoreham who's looking for him.'

'Really? I was going to ask D.I Crowther to liaise with the man from Shoreham but maybe it'd be better if you were involved; the possibility of a connection to your case is so obvious it makes no sense whatever for you not to have some involvement in their enquiry.'

'Am I to take the whole thing over from Shoreham or do you just want me to assist them instead of D.I. Crowther?'

'The latter; I want you to keep in touch with the D.C. who came over from Shoreham until things become clearer. Once we're sure there's a connection between the two cases I'll sort out 'who does what'. I've spoken to his boss already. '

'And you've informed D.I. Crowther and he's happy?'

'I didn't ask him if he was happy Foxy … you know Jack. Any way he has plenty on his plate.'

'Fair enough Sir, I'll get D.C Best straight onto it. He can work with the lad from Shoreham as he knows him. Groves and I will stick with Roz Sommerton.'

'OK … just keep me posted; I'll make sure everyone who needs to know, knows. Now … as this is likely to deprive you of Best for a while I'd better relieve you of some of your other less pressing cases and give them to one of the others.
Let me know which you can let go and if you've any problems with anyone refer them to me - not the problems - the people - you can look after the problems yourself!'

'Understood Sir.'

'What sort of progress are you making anyway?'

'Not much. My priority's finding and informing the victim's next of kin and getting her positively identified.'

'Haven't you tracked anyone down yet … her parents or her …'

'I have and I haven't. We're pretty sure who she is from photographs we obtained from her office; all we really need now is to have the body officially identified. I spent most of yesterday afternoon and evening, trying to find someone to do it … and failed.'

'You couldn't trace anyone?'

'Oh I did that alright; I found where her mother lived.'

'Lived?'

'Yes, when I got there she was dead.'

'Not murdered as well … Oh dear God, here we go … this is getting worse.'

'No not murdered Sir, not as far as I can make out anyway. She'd died of a heart attack two days ago apparently - a pure coincidence, though I'm not treating it as such. There were no suspicious circumstances reported but in view of what's happened to her daughter I'm keeping an open mind until the autopsy report comes in. In other words I'm letting the doctor sort it out'

'Doctor Moss?'

'I wish it was. He'd normally be the one but he's not in today I've just tried to speak to him - he's a stinking bad cold. I was with him a good bit yesterday as it happens, and I'm hoping he hasn't passed it on to me. The new assistant will be doing the job … a young Polish fellah.'

'Doctor Vladic?'

'That's him.'

'Have you contacted him to see how he's doing?'

'Not yet. It's still too early for those guys. I'll try at nine. But if he can confirm the mother really did die of natural causes we can write her off and concentrate on the daughter, because she was definitely murdered.'

'I thought you said the autopsy on her wasn't done yet?'

'Nor is it; I'm going on what Doctor Moss told me yesterday before his cold sent him packing. I'll let you know when we have a full report giving both the 'cause' and the 'time' of her death.'

'Well you seem to be well on top of it Foxy as usual, I won't detain you any longer. Just keep me in touch won't you - and do it daily.'

Reynard nodded, and by then all but smiling made his way back to join his team with his newly acquired 'possible suspect'. As he approached his office he heard Groves and Best laughing, and as he was in such high spirits himself, he deliberately let his smile fade. By the time he was behind his desk and about to sit down he'd an expression on his face which was positively glum.

Groves, who'd been caught by joking like this countless times before decided to play along and gave a quick sideways nod to Best who, not knowing Reynard as well, had been completely taken in. 'You alright, Guv?' he asked, leaning forward anxiously as Reynard flopped into his chair and began to moan.

'No, Constable Best,' Reynard replied, clapping his hands to his head, 'I am not alright. I am unwell, I am very unwell. You are to be re-allocated to work with your colleague from Shoreham, and Sergeant Groves and I are going to have to do all the leg work for the rest of this case.'

'Oh no!' exclaimed Groves, putting her hand to her mouth and looking convincingly shocked 'You'll have to get someone else in, *we* can't be expected to spend our time running backwards and forwards.'

Best, still not quite sure what was going on, sat down. For a moment there was silence. Then Reynard looked up; he was grinning. 'Don't look so worried Constable, we're exchanging a few old cases for a brand new suspect that's all.'

Best, even then not *quite* on the wavelength, breathed a sigh of relief. 'You had me worried for a minute, Guv. Who's the suspect?'

'Coffee first,' said Reynard, beaming again by then, 'and one or two of my 'little friends' I think … anyone else like a biscuit; I see you've already got coffee?'

'I'll turn into a cup of blinking coffee if I drink any more but I would like one of your 'little friends' if I may.' said Groves, 'and D.C. Best got up so early this morning he missed his breakfast.'

'Help yourself,' said Reynard in an exaggerated flash of generosity, 'while we run through what we've got. I see you both have files in front of you, let's take 'em one by one and see what enquiries we want to pass on. The Super says he'll relieve us of one or two if he can and by the way Constable you're to work with your friend from Shoreham until we see if his enquiry is coinciding with ours. Now what can we give away.'

Groves pointed to a file she'd put on Reynard's desktop 'What about the eighteen year old girl who turned up working in the supermarket.'

'Yes, he can have her.'

'And the pilfering at the Princess Eugenie Hotel?'

'It too.'

'How about the arson at Century Cabs?

'And that.'

'The PharmoChem drug theft?'

'Ah … you were working on it, weren't you? Did you get a chance to talk to D.I. Crowther as I suggested?'

'Not yet.'

'OK, we'll keep that one for the moment you've done too much on it for someone else to get the credit; just nudge it along when you get a chance. Right give me the other three files and I'll drop them on his desk later. Now … let's work out how we're going to tackle what we have left, and how we can use Constable Best's pal from Shoreham to help us while we're helping him. OK … all agreed. Right, back to yesterday; how did you get on down in Dorchester, Sergeant.'

Groves took a notebook from the inside pocket of her jacket and flipped through the pages until she got to the right one. 'I'm not sure whether I had a good day or a bad day Guv. I got some solid information telling us more of our victim, but I also got stuff which in my view all but rules out as a suspect the man with the horse box trailer - Mr Leslie Bowtell. Irrespective of the information I collected I can't for the life of me imagine why he'd hand in the purse if he was the killer. Surely if he'd murdered Roz Sommerton he'd have done his damnedest to distance himself from us not put himself directly in our hands?'

'Double bluff?' suggested Best.

Reynard nearly choked, 'Double what! You're reading too many detective stories! Carry on Sergeant.'

Groves, ignoring the dig Reynard had made at Best's expense, did as she was told. 'Yes … well,' she continued, 'Mr Bowtell has a riding school in West Overton, near Dorchester and on his way back there with the trailer he'd just bought from a man in Saddlecombe Basset he called in to see his sister, who's been ill recently. He eventually stayed the night with her and her husband. They live not a hundred yards from the Fyling Castle car park and, as her gateway was too narrow for him to get the trailer in, he left it in the car park until early yesterday morning when he picked it up and drove it home.'

'What about the car, his 4x4, what did he do with it during the night?' asked Best. 'Did he use it?'

'The car was standing on the drive at the side of his sister's house from seven on Sunday night until six on Monday morning. Being slightly narrower and much shorter than the trailer he'd managed to squeeze it in. There're loads of vehicles similarly parked in drive ways all along the road. No wonder the man didn't notice it on his way home from the pub.'

'Reynard scratched his chin and realised it wasn't as smooth as he liked it. 'OK Let's put him to one side for the moment.' he said, jotting down 'Razor blades' on his note pad and drawing ring round it. 'And the purse?'

'He found it in the trailer when he got home. I've left it in forensics for them to scan for prints and I hope to have it back later today. As to the contents … well … it was like her room - neat and tidy. There were no notes, no receipts, no credit card counterfoils, or anything like that, just a Visa card, a debit card from NatWest, her driving license and Press Card. She also had a whole bunch of business cards which are probably going to be the only things of any use to us. Everything was in the name of Rosaleen Sommerton. Yes, it was definitely the purse of the dead woman found in Fyling Castle car park; her press card had a photo on it.'

'Further confirmation our assumption of her identity is correct. Anyway, excellent - very good - but where does it get us?' asked Reynard, looking at each in turn.

'Not far?' suggested Best.

'One suspect less,' said Groves, 'so now we've only the one the Super's just given us.'

Reynard nodded thoughtfully. 'We'd better get cracking and find a few more then. Alright Constable, you can tell Sergeant Groves how we got on after she'd left for Dorchester … tell her what you and I discovered.'

Best, not expecting to have been asked was taken slightly by surprise. 'Er, yes … well we went over the flat again first Sarge, but when didn't find anything else of much interest we went straight on to the victim's mother's house in Upper Bedding to break the news.'

Groves nodded. 'How did she take it?'

Before he got a chance to answer Reynard asked Best if he hadn't already told Sergeant Groves what they'd discovered while *he* was in with Superintendent Bradshaw.'

Best shook his head. He'd thought of doing it but had held back in case Reynard wanted to make the revelation himself.

Groves watched their faces and began to titter, 'Come on Guv, one of us reveal something when you're not there … none of us would dare.'

Reynard grinned. 'Alright, enough joking … carry on Constable.'

'Well.' said Best. 'You'll never believe this Sarge; she was dead when we got there.'

'What … you found her dead?'

'No no we found she'd died on Saturday night, one day before her daughter. Natural causes apparently - heart attack.'

'Coincidence?' ventured Groves, knowing what would happen next.

'You're aware of my views on them Sergeant!' said Reynard, signalling to Best that he should continue.

'Yes … well,' Best said, 'we went round to the local nick in Steyning where we got confirmation Mrs Sommerton had been on her own when she died, but Sarge we're not convinced she had been. She was certainly *found* alone, lying on the kitchen floor of her bungalow, by the ambulance crew when they arrived, but who's to say there hadn't been someone with her before they got there.'

'Like who?'

'Like the man who'd called the ambulance and wouldn't say who he was, for example.'

'I don't like anonymous calls.' Groves said, hunching up her shoulders.

'It was from a telephone box at the end of her road.' Reynard added, 'And it's obvious, whoever made the call either found her dead, or was there when she died and didn't want to get involved.'

'Were you able to get into the house or talk to neighbours about what happened to her … or to Roz?'

'We borrowed the key and were in the house briefly, but we found nothing to connect the deaths.'

'Ah come on Guv there must be something, some little thing.' said Groves.

'I know, and we'll probably wind up taking Roz's flat and her mother's bungalow apart to find it.'

'So what's next?' asked Groves.

'We split I think. You make contact with the D.C. in Shoreham, Constable … what's his name again?' asked Reynard, as the phone on his desk began to ring.

'Furness,' Best replied, 'Dessie Furness.'

'Right, get hold of him and then you can … Hang on' he said, breaking off to pick up the handset and answer the call. 'Hello … Hello …'

Best pulled his mobile phone from his pocket. 'I'll give Dessie a bell when we're finished' he whispered to Groves, but she put her finger to her lips.

Reynard was also waving for silence. 'Right so we'll be working together. Fine .... D.C. Best, yes he's here with me now, you'd better come up and fill us all in.'

'Was that ...?' Best began to ask.

'Yeah ... speak of the devil!' said Reynard, replacing the receiver. 'It was your pal Furness. He's down at the front desk but he's coming up. Now, before he gets here we must decide on how we're going to ...'

'Why don't you wait to hear what he says before deciding?' Best asked, immediately wishing he hadn't when he saw the thunderous expression on Reynard's face. 'No perhaps not; he can sit at my desk until we're ready.'

'When you're in charge of the case you can do it your way Constable. In the meantime ... you and your friend D.C. Furness will do it *my* way. You can take yourselves up to the canteen and fill each other in regarding both cases. Sergeant Groves and I are going to have little chat with Marion Palfrey. We'll be back in an hour or so, and then we'll all sit down and agree what we're going to do next ... alright? Are you happy with that Constable Best?

Best nodded sheepishly, and remained silent.

112, Old Worthing Road, Brighton
Tuesday 16th February 2010. 10.35. a.m.

They found the chemist's shop easily enough and saw between it and the Old Worthing Road Sub Post Office a single door on which there was a well-polished plate reading Globe Newspapers Limited. The door was unlocked and they opened it and went in. Immediately in front of them was a steep rising staircase which they mounted to find they were on a small landing serving two rooms, the doors of which were open. One room overlooked the back garden the other, the one in the front, had a view of the traffic passing along the Old Worthing Road. A brief glimpse into the front facing room showed it to be unoccupied. In the other they found Marion Palfrey. She was sitting at a desk with her back to the window and facing a computer screen. She was on her own.

She looked up as they entered, presumably having been warned of their approach by the sound of their conversation as they'd climbed the stairs, but she made no move to get up from her chair.

'Miss Palfrey?' asked Reynard.

'Yes, you're the police aren't you? I still haven't heard from her, have you?'

Reynard smiled. 'Can you spare a few minutes. Sergeant Groves and I would like to talk to you to clarify a few things? I'm Detective Chief Inspector Reynard.'

'Wow, 'Foxy' Reynard. We've a file on you.'

Reynard couldn't disguise his amusement at the thought of *them* having a file on *him*, but before he got a chance to make any comment or get on with the delicate task of telling Marion her friend was dead, she was off again. 'I was reading it only the other day it's all about how you solved the … oh wait a minute … why are you here? Have you found her? … You have haven't you? … Oh my God she's dead … I didn't know … the policemen who came round yesterday for the photographs didn't tell me!'

Reynard, his jaws clamped together, nodded. 'We weren't sure then … Sergeant would you …'

'Sure.' said Groves, pulling over a chair to sit beside the already weeping girl.

'The thing is Miss, the body of a woman was found in the grounds of Fyling Castle yesterday. The provisional identification we've made using the description you gave W.P.C. Carville in the Police Station, and the photographs you handed to D.C. Best when he called round yesterday afternoon, makes us believe it is that of your friend Rosaleen Sommerton, or Roz as you call her. This has to be confirmed of course and as the only information we have about Miss Sommerton is what we saw in your statement, we will need your assistance.'

'Are on your own here?' asked Groves, pushing the tissue box towards her.

Marion puckered up her lips and began to wail.

'You are … so no one else works here just you and Roz Sommerton?'

Marion gave an almost imperceptible nod and pulled a tissue from the box. 'Mostly it's me; Roz is always out. There *is* another girl but she's out sick. '

'Perhaps I'd better have a word with your boss … tell him what's happened … see if he can send someone here to keep things going until you're a bit more composed. Would you like me to do that?'

Another nod.

'Horsham isn't it - your head office? What's the number? Who should I ask for?

Marion sniffed and wiped her eyes. 'Sorry ... I can't believe it … Roz … of all people … she was always on the go. Who did it? Have you found out who killed her? What did he … he didn't …?'

'Steady on Miss,' said Reynard 'we don't know what happened yet. Finding out's our next job. But we must sort you out first you're the only one so far who's told us anything about her. Now who should we telephone and what's the number?'

Half an hour later, with a temporary replacement for Marion on the way down from Horsham, and Groves driving Marion to her parents' house where she said she'd rather be than on her own in her bedsit, Reynard was prowling round Roz Sommerton's office in the front looking for clues. It was easy to see a common factor tying her office to her flat - tidiness - though the office was even more minimalistic. Painted in white and carpeted in serviceable graphite grey, it was so neatly laid out it might have been done with a tape measure. The equally spaced shelves opposite him each bore similar length rows of exactly the same sized red spined lever arch files - all similarly labelled. Three framed prints of Andy Warhol's portraits were hung in a dead straight line along the wall to his right, while against the one to his left a very healthy looking bright red poinsettia with a ribbon tied round it was precisely in the middle of a glass topped table. The desk and chair in the bay window, both modern and both looking new, had been placed in the centre of a large faux Persian Rug. It was all highly impressive and exactly what Reynard would have expected of the woman he was just beginning to know.

He got up and walked over to study the Warhol prints. 'You're not my sort of thing.' he said to the image of Michael Jackson but you, darling,' he whispered to Marilyn Monroe, as he tapped the glass with his knuckle, 'are a different matter altogether!'

He looked through a few of the lever arch and found they only contained newspaper clippings, notes she'd taken, and original texts of articles she'd written, none of which yielded anything to interest him.

He was about to turn to go back to the desk when a horn sounded outside and thinking it might be Sergeant Groves back from Marion's parents' house to collect him he went over to the window to see; but it wasn't her so he sat at the desk again and opened the A4 sized desk diary lying on it. It was the only thing there apart from the telephone. Very few pages had anything written on them, and even they told him little. Mostly they seemed to be reminders of commitments she'd already made or prompts to remind her of things she had to do in the future; and they were all brief.

The first was briefest of all, and was written on the page for the fourteenth of February, the day before she'd probably been killed. It consisted of one word, one letter, and six exclamation marks: 'Tell D!!!!!!' The second was equally cryptic; it looked like a reminder and was written on the page for the following day - Monday the fifteenth of February - the day she'd been found. It said 'Book Beech and Willows.' The third was well on into the year on the page for the twentieth of August; it said 'Remind Mum to be around.'

'Hmm, not much here to help us and no sign of a computer other than the laptop I saw in her flat.' mumbled Reynard, pulling out the top right hand drawer of the desk. It was full of pencils, ball point pens, paper clips, staples, and stationary items. The remaining drawers were empty bar a few things clearly to do with her work which he ignored, and a wallet full of visiting cards which he thought might be useful. He picked the wallet up and was about to go through it when he heard a car horn again and turned to look out of the window. This time it *was* Groves and she was letting him know she was back so he shoved the wallet of cards back in the drawer, picked up the desk diary, and went out to join her having locked the office and left the key back in the Pharmacy.

Sussex Police Major Incident Suite, Sussex House, Brighton Sussex. Tuesday 16th February 2010. 11.56. a.m.

The introductions were over and Groves, Best, and Furness, were seated facing Reynard across his desk. 'Right, let's review where are first so I know everyone's in the picture.' said Reynard, 'Sergeant - a summary please?'

Groves cleared her throat. 'Well we haven't made much progress yet, but then it's early days. We have the body of a young woman of thirty five or so who was found buried in a snow drift in the grounds of Fyling Castle. She's been provisionally identified as Rosaleen Sommerton, a.k.a. 'Roz' Sommerton, a freelance journalist contracted to The Globe and working from their Brighton sub-office. We have no autopsy report as yet so we have no firm time or cause of death but, as a working assumption, we believe she died of strangulation or a blow on the head some time on Sunday night.'

In the course of our enquiries we called on her mother, only to find she'd died the day before of a heart attack. The medical opinion regarding her death at this stage is she died of natural causes, but the coincidence of the deaths of these two women being so close together suggests much more investigation. So far, between us,' Groves continued, warming to her task, 'we've …'

'Hang on a moment Sergeant.' said Reynard, holding up a hand to stop her when D.I. Crowther unexpectedly stuck his head round the door.

'Alright for you lot,' said Crowther, 'I'm doing all your work and you're sitting here having a party. What are you - a debating society or what?'

'Go away.' said Reynard. 'it's *your* work we're doing. If you'd helped this poor man from Shoreham properly when he was with you yesterday we'd be able to get on with investigating a murder. Go and look at some files or whatever you do for a living and leave us real detectives to catch the villains!'

'Ooh, touchy isn't he.' said Crowther, a huge grin on his face. 'Alright I'll leave you to it, I've got a much more difficult one than you to solve anyway.'

Reynard laughed. 'What finding out who's nicking spaghetti hoops from the Princess Eugenie Hotel?'

'Very funny. No I'm looking for a body. I know who the killer is, but I've got no body.'

'Maybe we should put our cases together then, because we've got a body and no killer.'

'A tenner says my team scores first.'

Reynard looked at the three sitting before him: Groves, fit to burst, was holding back a laugh. Best, not entirely sure how to react without attracting criticism, was looking at the floor while Furness, unused to banter of this sort, appeared to be totally perplexed.

'Well?' asked Crowther. 'Are you on?'

'I'm on.' said Reynard, 'Now leave us alone.'

Crowther withdrew his head, and Reynard signalled Groves to continue.

'Right,' she said, 'so we're looking for a link between the deaths of Rosaleen Sommerton and her …'

'Let's stick to 'Roz'.' said Reynard.

'OK. We're trying to discover if Roz's mother's death had any bearing on Roz's murder. Our priority is to find and talk to family members and friends of either who we can trace - a simple enough job on the face of it but it won't be easy.'

'May I ask a question Sir?' asked Furness, hesitatingly raising his hand.

'You certainly may Constable, how else would we know if you were asleep or not?'

Furness risked a smile. 'What's the problem in finding the victims' relatives and friends?

'Aha,' Reynard replied, 'well you may ask … the mother was practically a recluse as far as we can make out, and the neighbour we spoke to said she had no visitors other than her daughter and seldom went out. As to relatives … well when we get down to 'phone and computer records and letters which we hope to find in the house, we might be luckier. As to her daughter, our murder victim in other words, it'll be a question of going through her flat and her things. We do know she was … what shall I say … gregarious, to say the least, she may have been more, she may have been flighty, a good time girl, someone who was up for anything. It's possible her adventurism took her too far.'

Furness shuffled about in his seat and then half held up his hand again. 'Sorry Sir, d'you mean she was a sort of high class call girl?'

'No I do not. I just mean she had a lot of men friends, men who were well heeled, men who wined and dined her in posh restaurants and took her on fancy holidays in places she'd never have been able to afford on her own. Mind you Constable … I could be completely wrong. We only have few scraps of flimsy and untested evidence so far. By the time we're finished we may have an entirely different opinion.'

Furness nodded. 'Thank you Sir, and what do we know about her father?'

'Nothing; he left them years ago we understand.'

'Will Dessie and I will be working together,' asked Best.

'Yes you will. ' Reynard replied, 'Your job will be to find something which ties the alleged rapist from Shoreham to Roz Sommerton. But first you'll have to discover if the allegation against him has any validity. If it hasn't he's unlikely to be of interest to us. Sorting that out has to be your first priority … only when we know if he's been giving other women a problem can we decide whether or not to treat him as suspect in the Sommerton murder. I know he wasn't to be found either at work or at home yesterday so once you've ascertained he's not been at work today make your way to his place in Armada Street and start from there - talk to neighbours, local shopkeepers, publicans, etcetera … you know the drill. And while you two are on that Sergeant Groves and I will be pressing on trying to gather additional information ready for our call on Marion Palfrey, at her parent's home, tomorrow morning. Tell them about Marion, Sergeant.'

Sergeant Groves pulled out her notebook. 'Marion Palfrey is a youngster who works in a junior capacity for the same newspaper as Roz. She was so shattered when we told her Roz was dead she all but passed out and had to go to her parents. Normally she lives alone in a nearby bed-sit. I'd already rung the paper's head office and informed them of Roz Sommerton's death and suggested Marion should be allowed to go home because she was shocked. They agreed and said they'd send someone straight away to 'man' the office until the end of the week. It was on the way to her bed sit Marion changed her mind and said she'd rather be with her parents. While I was there having a cup of tea with her and her mother she gave me some additional information which may be of consequence.'

'Which was?' asked Best.

'Yesterday, when she spoke to W.P.C. Carville, she says she felt she may have left her with the impression Roz was her friend, whereas in truth she couldn't abide her on a personal level. She only continued working with her because she was so brilliant at her job and knew she was learning a lot from her in terms of her work. This is an area I'll be more fully exploring with Marion later this morning. And that's as far as we've got.'

'OK' said Reynard, passing Groves the desk diary. 'Have look through this Sergeant; I took it from Roz's desk during the brief search I made of her office while you were driving Marion to her parents' home. See what you make of it and then pass it on to the others; I'd like their views too.'

Groves took the book and, laying it across her knees, turned the pages one by one while the others watched carefully; obviously the Inspector had spotted something and she didn't want to miss it. 'Hmm, only business things.' she said as she glanced at the entries Roz had made in January; but when she got to the two probably made at the end of the previous week, she paused. 'Couple of odd ones here, Guv.'

Reynard smiled encouragingly. 'Well?'

Groves quickly fanned through the rest of the book and passed it to Best. 'Well we have to find out who this 'D' is for a start.' she said, 'I'll ask Marion when I see her … and we have to find out why Roz wanted some trees when her garden's all paved. They're intriguing entries though … I suppose 'D' will turn out to be one of her men friends, someone she didn't want anyone in the office to know about…'

'By that you mean Marion?' asked Best, glancing briefly at the diary before passing it to Furness.

Groves shrugged her shoulders. 'Of course I mean Marion, who else?'

'I reckon these are just 'shorthand' reminders,' Furness suggested. 'Something she jotted down while she was on the 'phone. The exclamation marks after the 'D' could be doodles.'

'He's right.' said Reynard, 'Both entries may be 'shorthand' reminders. If you look in my diary you'll find similar ones. So what we have to do is find out who 'D' is and what the exclamation marks mean. We might ask Marion if she can throw light on either matter when we see her tomorrow.'

'Maybe the victim was referring to a book on Beech and Willow trees?' suggested Best. 'She could have been thinking of buying some for her mother - a birthday present perhaps - Mrs Sommerton's garden's enormous.'

Furness shook his head 'Beech and Willows sounds to me more like the name of a pop group … or possibly a pair of singers.'

'And what about the entry she made in August, no one's mentioned that.' said Reynard. 'Turn to the 20th and see what you make of what she's written there.'

Groves, embarrassed she'd missed it, snatched the diary from Furness's grasp, quickly turned to August and found the 20th, and then read out the short note written in Roz's hand. 'Remind Mum to be around.'

'Could mean anything.' said Best, 'Maybe it's a party she's planning.'

Furness had a better idea 'What about a wedding.' he said. 'Hers!'

Reynard rocked back in his chair with his hands clasped across his stomach and, with a look which was almost smug on his face, asked: 'Any other bids?'

Groves began to laugh. She'd been racking her brains for an answer in the hope of redeeming herself. 'I think I've have cracked it. It'll only take a telephone call to find out.'

'Don't tease.' said Reynard, 'what d'you think?'

'A baby.'

Reynard rocked forward again and slapped his knees 'Haha Haha - the first thought to come to my mind as well. And don't bother ringing Dr Vladic I've already done so; he'll check for pregnancy when he's doing the autopsy which, I hope, will be about now. In the meantime you and I Sergeant will go back and check over the flat and see if we can find any of Roz's neighbours to talk to, and Best and Furness can check that man's house in Armada Street. OK? Off we go then.' he said, draining his mug.

43, Armada Street, Brighton
Tuesday 16th February 2010. 2.50. p.m.

During the short drive to Armada Street Furness had given Best as much as he knew of the details of the alleged rape case. The man they were looking for he'd told him was Herbert McCloskey - a fifty year old bachelor, and night shift manager at Shoreham Power Station. He'd allegedly attempted to rape a young woman records clerk who worked on his shift. She'd made sexual harassment charges against him on a number of previous occasions, reporting him to her supervisor at least twice. Each time however, she'd naively failed to take a friend to witness her making the accusation and nothing, as far as she knew, had ever been done about either. The recent assault, according to her in the statement she'd made first thing Monday morning, had taken place during her shift on the evening before.

When Best had queried the fact it was a Sunday evening, Furness had told him the Power Station worked round the clock in a seven day three shift system, and that both parties involved in the alleged incident were on the second shift.

The woman claimed McCloskey had appeared unexpectedly in the office in which she was working, and she'd immediately sensed trouble in light of her previous experiences with him. He'd started by pulling her to him and trying to kiss her, but when she'd resisted he'd forced her back across her desk and begun ripping her clothing open. She'd screamed, she said, and luckily her cries had been heard by two male fitters doing maintenance work on the gas turbine. They'd come rushing up to the office to investigate and found her lying on her desk with McCloskey on top of her holding one of his hands over her mouth. The fitters had grabbed him and hauled him off her, but he'd struggled free of their grip and picked up a heavy metal framed chair. In the ensuing fight one fitter was hit by the chair, knocked unconscious, and suffered a broken jaw. The other, fearing he'd be next to be receiving McCloskey's attention, snatched a fire extinguisher from the wall and knocked McCloskey to the floor with it. While McCloskey was struggling to his feet, dazed, the uninjured fitter took the woman's hand and they ran off and hid in a small Spare Parts room behind the main turbine.

For a while they heard McCloskey shouting as he searched for them, but gradually the place went quiet. Unsure whether he was waiting for them or not, they remained in hiding for the best part of an hour before they risked coming out and calling the police. When a squad car arrived and a search got under way, it was soon discovered that McCloskey's car was missing from the car park. Assuming he'd gone home the police asked for his address, and the Administration Manager had to be hauled out of bed to get it. All in all McCloskey had had a head start of two hours.

'I was in one of the cars which went to his flat to arrest him,' Furness told Best, 'but there was no sign of him when we got there, and no answer when we rang his bell.'

'So you broke in?'

'We did; the place was empty. We put a temporary lock on and left; I have the key.'

'So now it's up to us to turn it over and try to work out where he's gone.'

'Right, but the question is - did he at any stage go to Roz Sommerton's and attack *her*?'

Best shook his head 'Two women in one night? Nah - I doubt it - too much of a coincidence, but don't tell Foxy I said so; he'll have a nanny goat if anyone mentions 'coincidences' again.'

'He's not a bad guy is he, your boss?' said Furness, taking the front door key from his pocket.

Best pulled his coat over his head to shelter himself from the falling snow and laughed. 'Yeah, as long as you …'

'Don't mention 'coincidences'!' replied Furness, grinning as he pushed the key into the Yale lock.

3A, Jutland Street, Brighton.
Tuesday 16th February 2010. 2.50. p.m.

The snow was turning to sleet, and Groves pressed herself against the wall beside Rose Sommerton's front door for shelter as Reynard tapped his pockets in search of the key.

'Shall I try the flats upstairs while you're looking round inside?' asked Groves.

'Yeah, good idea … call me on my mobile if you find anyone who knows anything and I'll join you.'

As soon as Groves had gone Reynard opened the door of Roz's flat and went in; it was freezing inside. 'Timer?' he said to himself, 'The heating'll be on a timer, and it'll be in an 'off' period during the day.'

He found the boiler in a cabinet beside the sink and, after spending a while puzzling out how it worked, he eventually managed to over-ride the programme. Soon he could feel the heat coming into the radiators and felt he dare take off his overcoat.

The laptop was standing beside the desk, and rather than risk the battery running down he found a suitable socket and plugged it in. Far from an expert, he did have enough rudimentary knowledge to discover she seemed to have little use for the programmes it offered other than the one for word processing - 'Word' - to which he went. On her desktop screen was a series of folders. One was labelled 'Globe', alongside it were others labelled: 'Drafts', 'Projects', 'Household', 'Personal', 'Financial', 'Downloads' and 'Other.'

He opened the 'Globe' file and found it contained what he expected: folder after folder of submissions which he assumed had been subsequently published in the newspaper. The 'Draft' file appeared to contain work in progress, while the one marked Projects only had as random series of notes on ideas for future work. The Household file had three folders in it: Gas, Water, and Electricity. The Financial file was empty - a good intention to make budgets and track expenses never fulfilled, he assumed. In the Download file he found films, music, and a variety of free and bought-in software relating to her television and her computer. The Other file was full of all manner of business letters, none of which he decided had much to do with her death. The Personal file was the one he concentrated on, going through every letter she'd written, but he still found nothing of interest. Next he turned to the internet and discovered the broadband connection was live. He made straight for her e-mail account and spent the next half hour reading every letter she'd received, or sent, in the previous six months. He was studying the notes he'd made on these when Sergeant Groves knocked at the door. 'How d'you get on?' he asked after he'd let her in.

'Quite well I think. I started with Pat McWilliam who lives in 3B with her husband Ed, and once I realised she'd information relevant to the case I asked her if we could have half an hour with her. She agreed, but as she'd just got out of the shower she asked if we'd mind waiting for twenty minutes. I said we would, mainly to give her time to recover from the shock she got when I told her what we're investigating. Is that alright with you?'

'Of course it is; what does she know?'

'It's not so much what she knows, as what she saw and heard outside on Sunday night.'

'Ah … sounds promising.'

'I just got the barest of details, but you're right.'

'Any others?'

'The Forsyths in 3C are away skiing in Austria and have been for the last ten days, according to Mrs McWilliam, so they were out of the country when Roz Sommerton was killed. I then tried the basement flats in the houses either side of Roz's. In 2A they told me they didn't know her and wouldn't recognise her if they saw her; in 4A I got a load of gossip from a rather overpowering woman of eighty, Mrs Tavish, who never stopped talking but knew nothing of Roz's recent movements,'

'We'll take armed back up if we have to go back to that one!'

'We might need it.'

'Anymore?'

'No. I was going to try the remaining flats in the houses on either side but somehow the time had slipped by and I realised Mrs McWilliam was about due, so I came back. How did you get on? Did you find anything we missed before? Did you see a bank file anywhere?'

'I saw one full of monthly statements in a desk drawer yesterday, but there's nothing on her laptop. Why?'

'I thought I'd take it back to the office and go through it when we're finished here.'

Reynard was about to answer when there was a knock on the door.

43, Armada Street, Brighton
Tuesday 16th February 2010. 3.14. p.m.

A quick look round was all they needed to conclude they were in rented accommodation. The flat, carpeted throughout with non-matching off-cuts in hideous colours was furnished with a mixture of cheap flat pack self-assembly stuff and a pair of bright orange sofas. The bedroom was in total chaos; the single wardrobe left half open. All that remained in it was an old sports jacket and two pairs of trousers, while in the drawers was only some underwear, much discoloured from frequent washing, and half a dozen pairs of socks. They found no shoes at all. The bed, which had not been slept in was in a rumpled state and covered with empty clothes hangers; obviously it was where he'd packed his cases. In the bathroom the airing cupboard was also open … and empty. In the kitchen/living room it was the same … a few loose papers but nothing else. It was obvious he'd gone for good.

'So what d'you think we should do, there's nothing here?' asked Furness.

'We'd better have one last look round and then we'll go; Foxy'll roast us if we miss anything. You re-check this room, I'll do the bedroom.'

The bedroom chest of drawers still yielded nothing, nor did the bedside cabinet or the bookshelf, but he unexpectedly struck gold when he went back to the wardrobe for a second time. He'd patted the trousers' pockets and the side pocket of the sports coat earlier and found nothing, but when he put his hand inside the inside pocket of the jacket when he went back to re-check it he discovered a piece of paper. One glance was enough - it was a receipt for three thousand five hundred and fifty pounds, written on a sheet of Basildon Bond writing paper and signed by 'Rosaleen Sommerton'

3A, Jutland Street, Brighton.
Tuesday 16th February 2010. 3.27. p.m.

I'll go.' said Groves, as she'd returned a moment later with a medium height well groomed silver haired sixty year old woman dressed in a black suit; she was so smart she looked as though she'd stepped out of a catalogue. 'Hello, I'm Pat McWilliam,' she said, leaping forward enthusiastically with her hand extended.

Reynard, invariably suspicious of heartiness, took it warily. 'Good of you to come Mrs … 'er … McWilliam … we're hoping you can help us. I'm Detective Chief Inspector Reynard of Sussex C.I.D. and we're involved in a murder enquiry regarding the death of a young woman whose body was found the day before yesterday up at Fyling Castle.'

'And you believe this poor soul might be Roz, that's terrible.' Mrs McWilliam replied.

'Yes … we think it could be her, though we've had no official identification as yet. Thank you for coming down anyway … we're trying to piece together her movements on the day of her death and it's in this connection we're asking …'

'I'll do my best. I did see her during the evening as I told the Sergeant here. It was about six thirty I think. Ed and I - he's my husband - were just leaving to go to The Feathers for a meal. We generally try to be there in time to catch the Early Bird Menu, it's very good value. Perhaps you've …'

'No, I've never been in the hotel Mrs McWilliam. Now … as to what you saw …'

'Oh yes sorry ... well, as I said, we were just leaving when Ed, my husband … oh yes I told you that … well anyway, we were on the front step and he was locking the door when he realised the snow was coming down heavier than he'd thought and he decided to go back to get his cap … he's a bit thin on top you see, and he feels the cold something shocking through the top of his head if it's not covered. You'd be alright though I expect Inspector; you've a fine head of hair on you. My husband on the other hand, is not so … '

'Yes, yes, Mrs McWilliam. What did you see?'

'I was at the top of the steps fully exposed, if you know what I mean.' she said, tittering at her choice of words.

'Yes, yes … exposed to the snow … what did you see?'

'Well Ed had shut the door behind him when he went back inside, so to keep the snow off myself I'd pressed myself as far back as I could against the front door and kept well under the canopy.'

'What I think Mrs McWilliam is suggesting,' Sir, said Sergeant Groves, '*is* because she was dressed in black and standing in front of a closed black front door, she probably wouldn't have been noticed by anyone passing by in the street.

'Exactly.' said Mrs McWilliam, 'And I was there for well over five minutes, freezing, while Ed searched high and low for his cap. Well,' she said, continuing to test Reynard's patience. 'he doesn't wear it very often.'

'And that's when you saw Miss Sommerton?'

'Roz, yes. A car drew up and the driver got out, a man … I think I've seen him there before. He went through her gate, under the step I was on, and knocked on her front door.

Now I'm not one to poke my nose into other people's business, you understand …'

'But you couldn't help overhearing their conversation?'

'Well … some of it … I heard her say 'Oh it's you, Geoff, I'm just going out.'

'And?'

'And nothing, they went inside and a minute or two later they came out again … together.'

'Yes …?'

'He was reminding her to look at something.'

'D'you know what it was?'

'No; but she said it sounded lovely from the brochure and she'd ring him with a few possible dates later in the week.'

'Sounds like he'd given her an invitation of some sort. Could they have been discussing a holiday he wanted to take her on? I believe she'd had a few glamorous ones.'

'It might have been, she went to Corsica last year with a friend, she told me. Huh, *'friend'* my eye. She went on a safari in Kenya the year before last with another. *I've* never even been to France … and you can nearly *see* it from here!'

Reynard grinned 'She was a lucky woman to have so many generous friends.'

'Oh I'm not saying she didn't pay her own way because she might have done. No, it was just the way she put it when she told me, I thought …'

'OK, Mrs McWilliam, what else did you hear?'

'Not much, I mean I wasn't listening it was just … well they were only a few feet away from me.'

'And so they didn't see you, yes, I understand. All the same you may have heard something which might be important. So what else did they say?'

'She said something about being sorry she couldn't spend more time with him, because she had to get on as she was late. They were back out on the pavement by then and next thing they were in the car and driving off.'

'In what direction?'

'Round the corner.'

'Left or right?'

'Left, towards The Feathers Hotel.'

'I see. Alright. Now as to the car: anything you can remember about it - its colour for example?'

'Well it was a big brute of a thing. Ed calls 'em gas guzzlers. I didn't really see the colour properly … only that it was darkish.'

'Hmm. What time was this?' asked Reynard. 'This is important so don't guess.'

'The clock was chiming the half hour when we first went out and it's five minutes slow, so it must really have been somewhere between six thirty five and twenty to seven when I saw them. Oh yes, and wait a minute there was another thing - it was an Irish car - it had an IRL sticker on the back.'

'Are you sure?'

'Oh yes, there were Irish people living next door to us a few years ago; they had a sticker just like it on their car. I remember it well.'

'Mrs McWilliam this is vital information you're giving us. Be sure to be as accurate as you can when you answer our questions, don't be tempted to say what you *think* you saw or heard. If you can't answer positively, say so. And please don't guess or embellish anything, it might mislead us.'

'I wouldn't do that, of course I wouldn't, Chief Inspector.'

'No I'm sure you wouldn't - I just want to make sure the evidence we collect is strong enough to stand up to a cross examination in court if we get there. We already have some information on cars which may have been involved and we need to check if what you tell us corroborates it or contradicts it. That's why accuracy is so important.'

As they'd been speaking they'd moved to the table and taken places facing each other. 'Right, let's get on.' said Reynard, 'Sergeant Groves has been taking notes of what you've told us so far and you can go over them with her once we've finished to check she's got it right. Is that OK with you?'

'Will I have to appear in court?'

'I couldn't say. It's not down to me; the DPP makes those sorts of decisions. Now back to the car for a minute. You say it was a large one … how large?

'Huge. I hate them big ugly things which …'

'Four wheel drive was it?'

'What're they?'

'Well like a Land Rover, for instance?'

'My nephew's got one like it - it's called a Shot Gun I think … daft name for car if you ask me.'

'Ah … I think you'll find it's Shogun! Yes those are big ones. OK and it was dark you say?'

'Dark yes, but not black - dark grey or dark blue more likely.'

'You didn't by any chance see the registration number … or any part of it even?

'I did as a matter of fact. It looked so strange on the back of a car.'

'What did?

'The PIN number of my credit card.'

Reynard sat back with a look of astonishment on his face. 'What?'

'It's funny you know, I can never remember it when I need it. I was in Tesco's the other day and … well it was so embarrassing …'

'Yes, yes, yes, Mrs McWilliam … but what's the number - what's your PIN number?'

'There were some letters in front of it.'

'Your number *please* Mrs McWilliam?' cried Reynard, on the verge of exploding.

Mrs McWilliam, unfazed by his outburst, pondered before answering. 'Oh … well … I don't know if I ought … Ed's always told me not to give my number to anyone else.'

Reynard began rubbing his knees and drew in a deep breath, always a very bad sign. 'We're not 'anyone else', Mrs McWilliam,' he said, slowly and deliberately, 'We're the police. This is a murder enquiry. We have to know - so tell us - what's your number?'

'Oh I suppose alright. It's 1,9,6,7, no it's not, it's 1,6,9,7? I never get it right, yes it's 1,6,9,7 … I was just about to tell you what happened in Tesco's ….'

'Does that sound like an Irish registration number to you Sergeant - a few letters followed by four digit number?'

'I wouldn't know, Guv, I'll have to check.'

Reynard turned back to Mrs McWilliam. 'Are you sure it was Irish?'

'Yes,' she replied. 'I told you; there was an IRL sticker on it.'

'OK. For the moment we'll take as being an Irish car ending with a four digit number. Anything else? What about the driver?'

'Well, apart from when he came round from the driver's side and went open her gate I didn't see his face, because he always had his back to me.'

'Age?

'Hard to tell from the little I saw of him … forty five maybe … or fifty.'

'Build?'

'Oh big … six feet at least, gauging by her height which is the same as mine. He was bulky, but it could have been his clothes of course, it was a cold night. I think his hair was short and curly … it looked a bit like yours Inspector but dark brown or black not grey, and that's about all really.'

Reynard drew in another deep breath and sat back in his chair with his arms folded, slowly nodding. And then he began to whistle quietly - in and out like a distant police car siren. 'Hmm.' he said finally, and straightened up again. 'We'll leave it there for now Mrs McWilliam, and thank you again.'

'I hope you catch him.' she said.

'And there's nothing else you can remember, which might be relevant to our enquiry?'

'Only one thing - he was carrying a big envelope in his hand when he arrived. He didn't have it when he left.'

'Ah, good we'll have a look for it. So there's nothing else you saw or heard?'

'Not really, they drove off as Ed and I were going down the steps on our way to The Feathers for our 'Early Bird'. It's a three course meal you know and only they charge seventeen pounds fifty and that includes …'

Groves put her hand up as though she was stopping traffic. 'Just a moment Mrs McWilliam, you said 'not really', why? Did you see her again later in the evening?'

'Well that's the funny thing Sergeant I did; it was very odd. Ed and I had had a drink in the bar as usual while we were ordering our meal, and we'd just gone into the dining room and been shown to our table when she came flying through the service door from the kitchen, raced past us as if we weren't there, and disappeared out into the foyer.'

Reynard thought for a moment. 'Yes, very strange, she must've been upset or pre-occupied.'

Mrs McWilliam gave her opinion more robustly. 'Or ignorant!' she said.

'And you never saw her again?'

'No, never. Just the twice: outside the house and in the dining room.'

'How much later was it when you saw her in the dining room?'

'Er … um … Oh Gosh … It was before seven thirty for sure because that's when the Early Bird last orders are taken. Say around twenty past seven.'

Reynard got up from the table and started to button his coat. 'Anything else Sergeant?' he asked, but Groves shook her head. 'Mrs McWilliam, do you want to ask us anything?'

'I don't think so Inspector.'

'Right you can go now if you like. The sergeant and I are going to look for the envelope. See yourself out will you … and thanks you've been very helpful. Oh one last thing … would you say Miss Sommerton was a friendly neighbour?'

'Friendly? Don't make me laugh. She was a stuck up little madam. No chance we'd ever have been good enough for her, she lived in a completely different world to the rest of us - a real high flyer. My Dad had a word for people like her - 'fast and loose'- he'd have called her. I don't know how many men I've seen her with since Ed retired and we came to live in Jutland Street, plenty anyway. I'm sorry she's come to such a horrible end but I'm not the slightest surprised at what's happened. I reckon she was asking for it. Posh as she made out she was, she was no more than a high class tart - there I've said it.'

'Hmm, a harsh judgement,' Mrs McWilliam' said Reynard. 'maybe it would be better to wait until all the facts come out. Anyway thanks once more, and once you and Sergeant Groves have agreed the notes she's taken, we're finished. You won't be going away for the next few days I suppose ... just in case we need to talk to you again?'

'Go away … in midwinter … me … not likely.'

'Fine, I'll say goodbye then.' said Reynard, making for the desk.

Ten minutes later, with the notes Groves had taken agreed in his hand and Mrs McWilliam gone, Reynard … having failed to find the envelope in the desk … was in the bedroom where he soon discovered the envelope under the jacket Roz must have flung on the bed. 'Changed her mind about what she was going to wear at the last minute I expect Guv.' said Groves, from the doorway.

'Tell me about it!' Reynard replied, picking up the envelope. On the outside was printed:

Just in case you're not in when I call, here's where I suggest. I hope it's better than where we stayed in September. I'll call you one evening next week if you haven't rung.

Inside the envelope was a small booklet entitled 'Things to do in Morocco' and a brochure for a hotel in Marrakesh. A date in June, followed by a question mark, had been written on the brochure with a felt-nibbed marker pen.

'So it looks as if Geoff was planning to take her on an expensive holiday.' said Reynard.

'And very nice too.' Groves replied, flicking through the heavily illustrated pages. 'It never happens to me, my fellah expects me to pay my own way.'

Reynard gave her a wry smile. 'Ah, but look where it got her.' he said.

'Yeah, you're right, Guv. I'm going to take her bank records back to the office and have a good go at them … what d'you think?'

'Good idea, Best and Furness can help you.'

'And another thing, when I was driving Marion Palfrey to her parents' house yesterday she asked me if I thought Roz was a prostitute. I said 'No' at the time but … well … I'm not so sure I was right now. The only difference I can see between a prostitute and a 'good time girl' is one gets paid in money and the other gets it in kind.'

Before Reynard got chance to make a response his mobile began to ring in his pocket. He yanked it out and held it to his ear. 'Hello … Yes it is … right … right. OK thanks - just as I thought.'

Groves raised her eyebrows. 'Who was that?'

'A message from Dr Vladic … Roz Sommerton *was* pregnant.'

'Ah.'

'Ten to twelve weeks, he says.'

'I wonder if Geoff knows?

'So do I. You'd better give Best a call; tell him and Furness to come round here right away, things are hotting up.'

43, Armada Street, Brighton
Tuesday 16th February 2010. 4.05. p.m.

Best put his mobile back in his pocket 'The boss wants us; we're to get a bottle of milk and a packet of Hobnob biscuits and join him and Sergeant Groves at Roz Sommerton's flat in the next street, pronto. Something's happened.'

'OK. When you tell him what you've found he'll think it's his birthday.'

'He didn't really believe there was a connection y'know. Never said it in so many words but I'm damned sure it's what he thought.'

'Well we've made one.'

'Yes I know we have, and it's in writing, but the trouble is the receipt's dated three months ago.'

'Why d'you think he paid her the money?'

'Ahhh … that's a job for the Governor … he's the one who does the deducing in our team … or so he tells us so. Hey, I've an idea … we'll pick up Roz Sommerton's bank records while we're round there, *they* could be worth checking.'

3A, Jutland Street, Brighton.
Tuesday 16th February 4.18.p.m. 2007.

D.C. Best's huge grin would have given the game away the minute he came through the door, but before he got a chance to reveal his startling news Grove came out with hers.

'A baby?' said Best. 'Blimey, that'll put the cat among the pigeons. But surely it'd hardly be enough to provoke a murder.'

The D.C.I. obviously disagreed. 'Really?' he said, 'Suppose a man thought he was the only one in a woman's life and found he wasn't. And suppose he was given to jealousy and bad temper, what then? They say 'hell hath no fury like a woman scorned' - but I think it's just as true with men and may well be a factor in this case; men do strange things when they're blinded by passion. Look … someone fathered Roz Sommerton's child … maybe someone else, who thought they should have done so, killed her in a fit of anger. Her having a child has got up someone's nose you mark my words, and we have to find out who he is. But it's going to be a huge task if what Marion Palfrey and Mrs McWilliam have told us is true … so we'd better get on with it. What d'you think?'

For a full minute there was silence; who was going to challenge a conviction so strongly put?

Groves broke the spell. 'You have it all worked out Guv, and I don't disagree with what you've said.'

'Nor do I.' said Best, not *daring* to contradict.

Furness gave the D.C.I.'s suggestion a more earthy endorsement. 'Well,' he said, 'she certainly put it about a bit.'

'No need for that,' said Reynard, 'but you're right. This woman liked living in the fast lane with men who had plenty of money to spend. We've heard about one in the last hour from a neighbour who witnessed him talking to her on Sunday evening and giving her an envelope containing an invitation to go on holiday with him in a very fancy hotel in Morocco. Finding him is our first priority … but there will be others, several of them I expect. We've got a motive now and I don't doubt we'll find more, but it's a good start so let's keep our eyes open for signs of disappointed boyfriends called Geoff.'

'Or Chef, don't forget the guy who sent her this rose.' said Groves pointing to the wilting flower in the vase.'

'Or her fiancé … whoever he is.' said Best, 'assuming he's neither Geoff nor Chef.'

Furness, quiet since the D.C.I. had criticized him, suddenly sat up straight. 'Say that again.'

'Assuming he's neither Geoff nor Chef.'

'When you first said it I thought you'd repeated yourself - 'Geoff' … 'Chef' … they sound much the same to me.'

'Well done you,' said Reynard, in a more conciliatory mood, 'you're absolutely right they *do* sound the same. So Mrs McWilliam - she's the neighbour we've been talking to - might have misinterpreted what she heard, and taken 'Chef' for 'Geoff'. Maybe there'll only be two men for us to find - Chef/Geoff, and the fiancé.'

'Hang on Guv,' said Best, 'what about Herbert McCloskey, we mustn't forget him.'

'True, but I doubt we'll find much to connect *him* to her … other than living round the corner.'

'I don't want to contradict you Sir, or top the information you've just given us about the baby, but we've got some news as well … look at this.' he said, handing Reynard the slip of paper he'd found in McCloskey's jacket.

Reynard looked at it for a moment, whistled, and passed it to Groves. 'How are we off for coconuts Sergeant?' he asked, 'These two men deserve a prize.'

Groves glanced at the note and grinned. 'So they do Guv, but the best we can offer them is a cup of tea, and we can't even do that unless they brought some milk.'

'Here y'are Sarge.' said Best, handing her a plastic supermarket bag, 'and I put in a packet of 'you know what's' for the Governor.'

'No, hold it.' said Reynard, 'we need to be in the office until we've sorted out where we're going. And in the meantime can anyone tell me why McCloskey might have paid her three and half thousand pounds?'

'He bought something off her.' suggested Best.

Groves stiffened a finger and pointed to the sky. 'A car.'

Reynard nodded, 'Just what was going through my mind. Right, McCloskey's *your* bird Constable Furness so you can find out what the registration number of his car is, and check its recent owners.'

'I have the number already Sir; I got it from security at the Power Station yesterday, and I put out an 'all stations' call for assistance in the hope someone would spot it.'

'Well done, now all we need to do is see if there's any reference to a car with the same Registration Number in Roz Sommerton's papers. Do it now, before we leave, D.C. Best can help you. If you find one, we've a definite connection and we can confirm Mr McCloskey as one of our possible suspects.'

Furness, who'd lost the thread of the conversation in all the excitement, held up his hand. 'Repeat who they all are again if you would please Guv.'

'OK,' said Reynard, 'So far we have the guy she was engaged to, or not engaged to, we'll call him 'the fiancé'; we have a man who refers to himself as 'Chef'; we have 'Geoff', assuming he's not sometimes called 'Chef' as well; we have McCloskey; and we have the new mystery man 'D', if he's not 'Chef' either … five men … let's go and find 'em.'

Furness who'd never been on a murder investigation before, shook his head. 'Blimey … five guys to find.'

Best started to move towards the desk 'I'll make as start on the car then …'

'Top drawer.' said Groves, there's a file in there marked 'Car' … try it. It's full of insurance reminders going back for years.'

Reynard waved his hand to stop them. 'No bring it back to the office instead. Once we're there I want D.C Furness to stick to locating McCloskey's car while you,' he continued, turning to Best, 'can help Sergeant Groves to find the *Irish* car we've heard about this morning. After that you can help her to go through the bank statements. But the cars are key to our investigation, if we locate them we may discover we've located two of the five suspects.

Now, before we go, see if you can spot a cardboard box or a suitcase and empty all the paperwork out of the desk into it. We'll examine the whole lot more thoroughly after we've tracked the cars and checked the bank statements. Why don't you go back with them Sergeant, you can fill them in with the rest of what transpired at the interview we had with Mrs McWilliam on the way. I'll make may own way to the office and I'll see you in an hour.'

The Showrooms of Paint and Paper Ltd, Ironmonger Street, Brighton, Sussex. Tuesday, 16th February 2007 5.00p.m.

Cathy Reynard emerged from the shop with a sigh of relief. 'I thought it would have taken longer bearing I mind how fussy you are.' she said.

Reynard looked at his watch and sighed. They'd chosen new wallpaper for the dining room, something he'd been putting off for months. 'You do it, you know about colours and designs.' he'd said, but she wasn't going to risk going down that road and leave herself open to criticism every time he went into the room. Instead she'd worn him down until he'd agreed to join her in the showroom so they could make their choice a joint one.

'Have you time for a cup of tea?' she asked.

'No … well alright,' he said, 'but a quick one.'

They went into 'Fletcher's', an old fashioned tea room renowned for its scones - a favourite of Cathy's.

'How's it going?' she asked.

'The case? Alright; we've had a bit of luck this morning which might bring us forward a few steps.'

'They were talking about her in the hairdresser's, surprising how so many women read her column, and they all seemed to know a lot about the life she led.'

'Oh really, what were they saying?'

'You know, how she was …

'A tart?'

'No, more like 'full of life'.'

'Not any longer.'

'Oh *men*! You're all the same. A man can go out on the town and he's great. When a woman does the same she's a tart, you know it as well as I do.'

'Do I? Well maybe, but from what we've heard so far she was, at the very least, fickle and feckless. In fact we're on the track of five men she's been going out with at the same time. She might even have taken money from some of them but even if she didn't, she took presents like holidays in Morocco and you can guess what they probably got in exchange.'

'Chauvinist! That's lucky, not feckless.' said Cathy smiling. I wish someone would take me to Morocco.'

'Well it won't be me … all that funny food … nah … we'll go to Falmouth. You like Falmouth.'

'Do I? Oh good … I'd probably like Morocco as well if I got the chance. That's the difference isn't it, between people like us and people like her. We always do what we always do … whereas she did *whatever* she wanted, *whenever* she wanted, with *whoever* she chose … and why not?'

'Nothing's wrong with it, Cathy, but look where it got her. Any way I must be off, they'll be waiting for me. I'll try to be home by seven.'

'Like you always do … only you always don't!'

Sussex Police Major Incident Suite, Sussex House, Brighton Sussex. Tuesday 16th February 2010. 6.14. p.m.

As D.C.I. Reynard got to the top of the stairs he bumped into D.I. Crowther coming out of Superintendent Bradshaw's office. 'Did you find your body Jack?' he asked.

Crowther, his glasses in his hand, squinted to see who it was. 'Oh it's you, Foxy. No I haven't, how are you doing?

'Alright. How d'you come to lose it?'

'It got swept away.'

'By what?'

'The sea. By the way … he's looking for you.'

'The Super?'

'Yes, and I wouldn't keep him waiting if I were you, he's in a shocking mood.'

'Is he? I'd better go and cheer him up then.'

Superintendent Bradshaw was sitting at his desk studying a file when Reynard went in. 'Good evening, Sir,' he said. 'I believe you wanted to see me.'

'I do … are you going back to your desk.'

'I am, Sir … why?'

'Jack Crowther's left this behind,' he said, 'would you hand it to him on your way past.'

'Sure, anything else?'

'Yes, I want to know how you're getting on. I've had the Chief Constable rattling my cage all day long; he plays golf with the owner of The Globe unfortunately and he's asked me to keep an eye on the enquiry. Bloody cheek … as if I don't keep an eye on all of them. But we don't want to get on the wrong side of him with these staff cuts in the pipeline so I'm going to humour him. Make sure you keep me up to date twice a day, and every time you sense or get a break-through … ring me. I'll be relying on you so don't let me down.'

Reynard paused before answering; he too needed to play the game the right way. 'Right Sir, will a verbal report do?'

'Verbals will be fine. Now what have you got?'

'Confirmation you're not losing your deductive skills for a start.'

'Go on.'

'The man from Shoreham Power Station, Herbert McCloskey, has a positive connection to Roz Sommerton as you surmised. He's is one of five possible suspects we've uncovered and are now tracking down with the intention of questioning them.'

'Splendid. You've made my day … what next?

'The case is broadening out, Sir. Everyone we speak to seems to wind up giving us another lead to follow. If we don't watch out we'll run out of legs.'

'I can't spare you anyone else if that's what you're after.'

'If I can keep D.C Furness, the lad from Shoreham, until the case is wound up, it'd help.'

'You can have him until the end of the week. I'll tell his superior myself.' said the Superintendent, 'And don't forget to give D.I. Crowther his file back.'

***

'Ah, I wondered where that had gone.' said Crowther, as Reynard dropped the file on his desk.'

'*Losing* a file, *losing* a body! Jack, you're definitely losing it yourself, it's no wonder the Super's going hairless.'

'Oh shut up.'

'Charming!' said Reynard, as he left for his own office where the rest of the team were waiting for him.

'Good timing, Guv.' said Groves. We're just about ready. D.C Furness has spoken to the insurance company Roz Sommerton was with and they told him McCloskey had switched to them when he bought her car. And the DVLA office in Swansea has confirmed he *is* currently the registered owner of the car formally owned by 'Rosaleen Sommerton'. He's already put out an 'all stations' alert for this vehicle, so we'll just have to wait and see what comes up in the next day or two.'

'Good. And what about the Irish car?'

'I rang the Department of the Environment in Dublin, which is the authority for car registration in that area of Ireland, and they told me there are no Irish registration numbers anything like the combination Mrs McWilliam remembered. Irish registrations for several years now have started with two numerals indicating the year of initial registration, one or two letters signifying the county or city of initial registration, and up to four numbers issued in order of registration. So it seems Geoff's car's not an Irish one, despite the IRL sticker. The only thing they could suggest is that the car is bearing a UK personalised number plate. Such plates are not available or valid for 'Irish' cars.'

'Damn,' said Reynard, 'we should have asked her if the plate had a white or yellow background; Irish ones are white, I'd forgotten. Anyway there's no need now, so it looks like the car Mrs McWilliam saw might be owned by a well-built six foot six Irishman called Geoff, who lives in England and drives an English registered dark coloured 4x4, of unknown make with an IRL sticker on the back. It's better than nothing.'

'I rang Mrs McWilliam while you were in with the Super and asked her if she'd thought of anything else after she left us, which was lucky because she had. On consideration she thinks the car she saw was fairly new, and when her husband found a few pictures 4x4's on his computer she thought the one she saw Roz getting into could have been a B.M.W.'

'Blimey Guv,' said Best, 'mug shots for bloody cars, what next?'

'It just goes to show,' said Reynard who, without bothering to explain what he meant, added. 'So send out another 'all stations' for this vehicle as well. Let's keep our fingers crossed and hope at least one of 'em will be spotted. OK … we'll let the cars stew for the moment and move onto something else.'

'I ought to get back to Shoreham.' said Furness.

'You're with us until the end of the week;' Reynard replied, 'I've just had it confirmed by the Super who's spoken to your Sergeant again. Right, if that's all, I'm off to the mortuary … write your reports up and … Sergeant … have a stab at getting everything on the display board before you leave … and see if you can start drafting out a time line.'

Brighton and District Mortuary,
Lewes Road, Brighton.
Tuesday 16th February 2010. 6.38. p.m.

Doctor Vladic went over to meet Chief Inspector Reynard when he saw his face at the glass panel of door. He'd both hands held up; one had scalpel in it the other a pair of blood covered surgical tongs. He looked as though he'd been stopped in the middle of conducting an orchestra.

'You got my message?' Vladic asked.

'About the pregnancy? Yes I did.'

'Roughly ten weeks I'd say.'

'Strange Doctor Moss never spotted it.'

'Not really; she wasn't very big.'

'Here we go, closing ranks?' thought Reynard.

'I've examined the stomach contents and it looks as though her last meal was a salad sandwich; one she'd made herself at a guess, as the skin was still on the cucumber. It was eaten a couple of hours before she died. This and other indicators lead me to believe the time of death was between eight and nine on Sunday night.'

'Excellent, and the cause of death?'

'I believe Doctor Moss already suggested a blow on the head, and I agree.'

'Not strangulation.'

'No. I have no doubt the bruises on her throat are less significant than the head wound.'

'How d'you think it occurred?'

'It was delivered by something with an edge.'

'A cutting edge?'

'No a blunt one, more like the edge of something rounded: a stone or a metal rod or bar. There was no residue in the wound so I can't help you any more on that score.'

'So she was hit with something? Hmm.'

'Yes, possibly, but she could also have fallen against something, say the edge of a door, or a kitchen counter top, even a metal or wooden hand rail.'

'It's take your pick then?'

'I'm afraid it is; there are countless ways she could have sustained such an injury.'

'Fair enough. Anything else?'

'Yes, I had another look under her finger nails and found a small sliver of skin under one of them.'

'Oh good; a sign of a fight of some sort? Doctor Moss said there wasn't anything under her nails when I asked him.'

'I thought the same yesterday when he and I gave the body a cursory examination, but we were wrong thank Goodness, and I've sent it off for DNA analysis. Let's hope we get lucky and find a match on the records.'

'Sure. And even if there isn't one the DNA will still give useful confirmation once we have him.'

'Or her.'

'Or her, true. Could a woman have done it?'

'Chief Inspector, you are the detective.'

'Will Doctor Moss be in tomorrow, it's not like him to give in?'

Vladic smirked but didn't answer; obviously he didn't believe Moss's 'bad cold' story either.

'Right, I'm off.' said Reynard, touching his forehead in salute. 'Let me know when the DNA results are in.'

He was home in fifteen minutes, at two minute to seven; Cathy nearly dropped.

Wednesday 17th February

Sussex Police Major Incident Suite, Sussex House, Brighton Sussex. Wednesday 17th February 2010. 7.54. a.m.

Groves was already in and writing stuff on the display wall when Reynard arrived. Best and Furness were right behind him and the whole team was sitting round Reynard's desk, each with a cup of coffee in their hand, before eight o'clock.

'Big day today,' said Reynard, 'we've a lot of loose ends to tighten up. Now … overnight thoughts … Sergeant Groves first.'

'I lay awake for ages thinking of this Guv, and a few things are bothering me. First, we really don't know enough about our victim. We're jumping to conclusion by labelling her 'fast and loose' and all but blaming her for her own death like Mrs McWilliam did when she said Roz was a 'tart' and 'asking for it'. I believe it's dangerous for us to assume such until we know more of her.'

'For what it's worth Sergeant, her reputation of being a 'tart' as you call it, was being discussed in a conversation my wife overheard yesterday in her hairdresser's. A number of women who were there at the same time she was, were discussing the murder.'

'And what did they say?' asked Groves.

'Well according to Cathy they saw her more as 'adventurous' than 'grasping', and Cathy agreed with them. I think you have good point though … maybe Marion Palfrey, who you and I are going see again shortly, might give us a different perspective. And second?'

'Second, I think we should go through her mother's house more thoroughly to see what we can find about the Sommerton family as a whole.'

'I was going to say we should go back to Mrs Sommerton's house too.' said Best. 'We only gave it a quick examination last time, didn't we?'

'Noted.' said Reynard, 'What about you D.C. Furness … any enlightening thoughts?'

'I'm an enthusiast regarding cars Sir,' he said, still wary of risking addressing Reynard as 'Guv'.

'And?'

'And I'm involved with loads of other guys with similar interests. I'd like to study the photos taken in the car park and spend some time with a tyre expert identifying the make of the cars we're looking for.'

'If *he's* going to do the cars, *I'll* get on with the papers we picked up.' said Best.

'Well I'm happy if you are. Excellent,' said Reynard, 'and the Sergeant and I will talk to Marion Palfrey again. OK? Chop, chop, let's get on with it!'

'The wall, Guv?' asked Groves. 'I didn't get time to do much last night.'

'Leave it until we've seen Marion. I got the time of death from Doctor Vladic and you'll be able to work back from that when we're back here later. All done? O.K. let's go … we'll take your car this time Sergeant.'

12, Cedar Gardens, off Worthing Road, Brighton, Sussex. Wednesday 17th February 2010 10.05. a.m.

Marion opened the door and let them in, and once the pleasantries were over and she'd introduced her mother and her father who'd stayed off work specifically to support her, they went into the front room where Mrs Palfrey had placed a tray of coffee and biscuits.

'Do you see what I see Guv?' said Groves, as she sat down next to Marion on the sofa.

'Excuse me Inspector,' asked Mr Palfrey. 'Do we stay or what?'

'It's alright if you stay, and alright if you don't Sir,' said Reynard, 'why don't we let Marion decide.'

'You and Mum go Dad, I'll be fine.'

As soon Mr and Mrs Palfrey had left the room Reynard began asking questions but Groves, seeing Marion's continuing discomfort, intervened. I think Marion's still not quite herself yet Guv, shall we have our coffee first?'

Reynard took the hint. 'Yeah, why not … you two take a few minutes to get to know each other and I'll go over my notes again.'

The look of relief on Marion's face was instantaneous, and for about five minutes she and Groves quietly chatted to each other about her job and her interests.

Every now and then Reynard would look up from his note book, and when he sensed Marion had emerged from her defensive shell, he gave Groves a discrete nod. Groves answered with an even more discrete one and then got down to business.

'I expect you've been giving plenty of thought to what we might ask you Marion.' she said, 'so, rather than throw a load of questions at you, why don't you tell us in your own words how you got on with Roz, and we'll take it from there?'

Marion nodded, started to speak … then stopped.

Groves guessed her problem immediately: she was torn between loyalty to her colleague, and opening the cage and letting everything come out; the interview had stalled before it had really started.

'Look Marion,' said Groves, in an attempt to re-assure her, 'nobody likes telling tales about their friends. We know you feel uncomfortable about speaking openly when Roz isn't here to defend herself, but if we don't have the full picture we'll never find who killed her. If you want to express your loyalty to her, help us to find who did this dreadful thing.'

'I know.' said Marion, forcing a grin so barely formed Reynard missed it.

Groves didn't though, and she leaned forward and took Marion's hand. 'It's alright, take your time.'

Marion sniffed back a tear. 'Alright, where do you want me to start?'

'Why don't you begin by telling us about your job and how it fitted in with hers? You were going to the exhibition together for example; did you often work in tandem?'

'No hardly ever, and I've no idea why she asked me to go to this one with her. She wasn't a sharer by any means, she wanted the credit for everything. To tell you the truth I thought twice about agreeing to go with her in the first place, but I wanted to see the exhibition and to be honest it seems a good chance to get in without paying.'

'So you agreed at the risk of ….'

'Of being bossed around all evening … yes, and I'd probably have regretted before the night was out.'

'Is that what she was like … bossy?'

'All the time … and she wasn't an employee like me, so theoretically she'd no right to do it to me.'

'Very annoying.'

'Yes, but she didn't care as long as she was the top one. I was going to leave but then I thought 'Why should I? I like my job'. It was just when she stuck her nose in and gave *me* orders to suit *her*, or sent me off on stupid errands, I got really fed up. I can't tell you how often she had me in tears and never even noticed. And when she did, do you know what she'd say … 'Stop snivelling!' That's the sort she was … hard and heartless, always pushing herself forward at my expense. I could have killed … oh no I didn't mean it.'

'Don't worry I understand. What did your other colleagues think of the way she carried on?'

'There are no other colleagues apart from the junior, and she doesn't do much yet, she's new. There really just Roz and me. Do you want more coffee?'

'Not for me thank you.'

'What about you inspector, d'you want any more coffee?' Marion asked, looking across to Reynard who'd retreated into his notebook and seemed to be taking little notice of the conversation.

'Er … oh … no thanks I'm OK, you two carry on. Don't forget to ask Marion about Roz's social life Sergeant.'

Marion laughed. 'She did the same in her spare time as she did in her working time.'

'Oh yes, what's that?'

'She chased men.'

Reynard, who oughtn't to have been surprised at Marion's comment in view of what he'd previously said himself, lifted an eyebrow - a little mannerism he'd practised to perfection. 'Well … you're frank I must say!' he said, 'tell us about some of them.'

Groves, worried Reynard had come in too soon, sat back with her clasped hands in her lap and waited for the tears. But they never came; Marion had been given a way in and was soon in full voice. 'Oh,' she said, 'she often had two or three boyfriends on the go at the same time. It was amazing the way she juggled them. She even involved me a few times, getting me to tell stories to get her off the hook. I don't know how she did it or why it didn't all somehow unravel.'

'Maybe it did.' said Reynard, quietly.

'You mean one of them … oh surely not.'

'What if one of them discovered he was being 'two timed' after spending a load of money on her? Who knows what'd happen then? There are countless examples of women killing men who rejected them … who's to say men don't do the same? said Reynard, hardly stopping to catch his breath.

'Oh well,' Marion conceded, 'maybe you're right … you probably are … what else do you want to know?'

Reynard got up from the arm chair and went over to look out of the window. The snow was swirling in every direction and beginning to build on the tops of the gate posts.

'What do we want to know? Yes, well we want to know everything Marion, absolutely everything and, thanks to you, I sense we're getting somewhere so just keep going on as you are, you're doing fine.'

'Really? But I still can't believe it's one of her men friends who did it.'

'Did you ever meet any of them,' asked Groves. 'or did you just hear her talking about them?'

'I never met them; never actually spoke to any of them. Oh wait a minute, yes I did … I spoke to one of them on the phone once, but I never met him. And I saw another one once, out of her office window when he came to collect her. Roz spotted me looking down on them as she got into his car. She was furious when she came in the next day … said I was spying on them and told me I was too nosey for my own good. I wasn't doing any harm, I was just curious.'

'Can you remember any of their names?'

'One was a soldier, he was lovely; in fact they were all lovely, she made sure of that.'

'How d'you mean … only chose good looking ones to go out with - is what you're saying?'

'She used to boast about it: 'If they don't come up to my standard they've no chance, she'd say.'

'And what *was* her standard?'

'Oh I don't know Mr Reynard - big, strong, smart, and handsome, I suppose. She was more interested in their looks than anything else.'

'More than their money?'

'Men used to give her wonderful presents … expensive ones, and took her to amazing places but to be honest I don't think having money was as big an issue for her as appearance and personality.'

'Some people seem to think otherwise.' said Reynard remembering the conversations his wife had overheard.

'What about their names? asked Groves.

Marion thought for a moment before answering. 'The only one I'm sure of is 'Geoff?' she said, 'I spoke to him once on the telephone, taking a message for her.'

'Irish is he?' asked Reynard, hopefully.

'He might be; I'm not good at accents.'

'So he didn't say Begorra!'

'No of course he didn't.'

'Sorry I was joking. And he wasn't the one you saw picking her up in his car?'

'No, that was the soldier I believe.'

'What sort of a car did he have - a big one?'

'I don't know - it was just a car.'

'What about Geoff's car, did you see *it*?'

'No, I just spoke to him on the 'phone.'

'Hmm.'

'You didn't say if you wanted more coffee Mr Reynard, I'm having one. And what about you?' she said, turning to Groves. 'You didn't say either?'

'Yes I will thanks.' said Reynard, 'It's nice coffee.' But Groves shook her head.

'I told you yesterday about the one I thought she might be engaged to didn't I?' said Marion, as she topped up the two cups. 'He's local I think, but I don't know his name and I've never seen him. All I know is he's something to do with the building trade.'

'A builder eh, I wouldn't have expected one of them? Tell me why you think she was engaged to him - something to do with a ring wasn't it?'

'Yes a ring on her engagement finger but it wasn't a proper engagement ring not with diamonds or anything. She used to always wear it all the time when I first met her, which was about eighteen months ago now, but recently she's stopped.'

'Stopped wearing it?'

'Yes and then about a fortnight ago, for a few days only, it was on again. It was a lovely ring - gold with a sort of rose embossed on it.'

'So you might say it was an 'on and off' engagement?'

'Yes it seemed to be. Daft isn't it? He helped her when she had a new bathroom put in but he mightn't have been an actual builder, he could just have been good at DIY like my Dad. '

'Did you ever hear Roz mention his name or where he lived or worked?'

'No, I don't think so.'

'He wasn't called Herbert by any chance?'

'Herbert! … No. She'd never have got engaged to man called *Herbert*.'

'She sold her car to a man called Herbert McCloskey, I wondered if it was him.'

'You mean the Fiesta, that was months ago. She's got Audi now … used to have an Audi I suppose … oh …'

Groves pulled a tissue from a packet in her handbag and gave it to her. 'I think Marion's had enough for the moment Guv.'

Reynard nodded. 'Yes, yes, I know … just one or two things more and then we'll go. You've told us about the fiancée, the soldier, and about Geoff. Are there any others we haven't spoken about?'

'Just Dimitri.'

'Dimitri?'

'Yes, he's a chef.'

Reynard's eyes nearly popped out of his head.

'Have I said something?' asked Marion.

'You never mentioned him before.'

'Well you kept asking me about the others. I was going to but you kept on about the cars. Dimitri works in The Feathers Hotel, he's the head chef.'

Groves quietly smiled to herself when she saw the look on Reynard's face. Reynard wasn't smiling though, he was tapping his finger tips on his knees he was so excited. 'Oh my God Sergeant we got it all wrong ... the 'Chef' who sent the rose wasn't 'Geoff' at all, it was Dimitri.'

Groves took her time in answering because she wasn't entirely convinced he was right. 'It's a possibility but let's not jump to conclusions.'

Reynard tried to laugh off what he saw as his misinterpretation of the names by making a joke of his apology. 'Typical … typical, I've done it again.' he said, shaking his head and sighing then holding out his hands palm upwards in a plea for forgiveness. 'Sergeant Groves is going to give me a right 'you know what' when we get back to the office.' he said to Marion, behind his hand and winking. 'She won't forgive me for not letting you tell us everything at your own pace, I'm sorry. What else were you about to say?'

'Not much really, Mr Reynard' Marion replied, clearly amused at the turn of events.

Reynard gave a flick of his head which Groves took to be another 'go ahead'.

'This Dimitri sounds an interesting sort of change for Roz,' she said, 'what do you think she saw in him?'

'I don't know, but you can be sure it'll have more to do with his looks than his money or his cooking!'

'Did she talk about him much?'

'She never talked about any of them much.'

'D'you know if Dimitri has a car?'

'No, I've no idea.'

'Have you ever met him?'

'I've never even been in into the hotel where he works … and no, I've never met him. I wouldn't have known anything at all about him if I hadn't overheard … well you know what our offices are - the doors are always open - anyway I heard her talking to him on the 'phone once and it was obvious from what she said they were seeing each other, if you know what I mean.'

'Oh, like that was it? Any idea what the conversation was about - a date I suppose?'

'No, it was about money, a loan of some sort I think, but whether he was borrowing and she was advising him, or she was borrowing and he was advising her, I couldn't make out.'

'This sounds promising Guv,' said Groves.

'Indeed it does.' Reynard replied.

Groves gave Marion a wink, 'Guv, this young lady's done well for us today but she's tired now. Why don't we leave her to rest - we can always come back again, or see her in the office.'

Reynard needed no persuading; he'd plenty to think about. 'Yes, alright, good idea, and thank you Marion you've been most helpful It's been a very productive meeting … we'll keep in touch.'

'Sure.' said Marion. 'I'll be in the office at nine tomorrow morning.'

As they walked to the car, highly delighted at the morning's outcome, Groves began to smile. 'Why don't we drive round to The Feathers Hotel for lunch, Governor? We can see Dimitri at the same time.'

'I hope you're joking,' said Reynard, fearing she wasn't.

'Don't worry Guv, I am; we can have lunch in the canteen and pay Dimitri a visit this afternoon.'

Sussex Police Major Incident Suite, Sussex House, Brighton Sussex. Wednesday 17th February 2010. 11.50 a.m.

D.C. Best and D.C. Furness were sitting facing each other across a table outside Reynard's office; each had a cardboard box beside him. Best's still contained some of the files taken from Roz Sommerton's flat. He'd been slowly going through them since Reynard and Groves had left to interview Marion Palfrey, taking them out one at a time and reading them from cover to cover. Each one as he finished it was passed to D.C. Furness who, having also read it, left it to one side for the D.C.I. to see or put in the other box for return to the flat.

'How're you getting on?' asked Reynard.

Best put down the paper he was reading. 'We're over three quarters of the way through.'

'And …?'

'And we've only found a few things of interest: a copy of the receipt she gave McCloskey for the money for the car, and three movements of cash which might need looking into in more detail.'

'Sounds interesting what are they?'

'The first is a letter from the National Savings and Investment Office which must have been attached to a cheque for ten thousand pounds she'd won with one of her Premium

Bonds. The second is also from them and it had enclosed a cheque for ten thousand pounds arising from the sale of part of her holding. The third is a bank statement showing the deposit of the two cheques totalling twenty thousand pounds and it's followed shortly afterwards by an entry showing a payment by cheque, number 000367, of twenty two thousand pounds. The payee according to her statement is 'Papagos' but, when we found the stub in her cheque book she'd written 'Dimitri Epicurus' and dated it 2nd January this year. It went through her account on the fifth. There's nothing we've found so far to indicate what she bought.'

'Brilliant.' said Reynard 'Well done, it ties up with something we got. Dimitri is the chef at The Feathers Hotel and he's also one of Roz Sommerton's many boyfriends, probably the one she refers to as 'D' in her diary. From what you've discovered we now know his surname is Epicurus. We also know from the bank statement that he appears to be trading as 'Papagos'. I think a quick bite in the canteen while we bring you two up to date re Marion's interview is indicated then, after lunch while you finish checking the papers, Sergeant Groves and I will slip round to The Feathers Hotel and have a chat with Mr Dimitri Epicurus and see what he has to say for himself.'

'What about the wall and the time line, guv?'

'With so much changing Sergeant I think it'll be better if you leave it until after we've seen Epicurus, you might have plenty of gaps to fill in then.' said Reynard, 'Come on, I'm ready for my grub.'

'Having something to eat before we go is fine by me Guv, but I doubt if Mr Epicurus'll be free until lunch in the hotel is over assuming he really is the chef. I'd say we'd be better calling on him after three.'

'You're right,' said Reynard, 'why don't you do your stuff on the wall after all while I go and have a chat to Doctor Moss about the time of death which I got from Doctor Vladic last night on this bit of paper. We can have lunch later.'

'I thought Doctor Moss was out 'sick''

'I saw him going into the Super's office as we came in just now so he's obviously better. It's not that I don't trust Vladic's judgement, but I'd like to have Doctor Moss's views as well, especially regarding the pregnancy and the possibility of matching the DNA of the foetus to some material Vladic found under one of the victim's finger nails.'

'To see if the father of the child is her killer? Surely he can't do that … sample a foetus.'

'I've no idea which is why I want to get Doctor Moss's view; he's been at this game a long time, he'll know the ropes. Look, if it's legally possible we ought to do it. We can make out own way to the hotel; I'll meet you in outside at three. OK?'

'At three, right … I'll be there.'

Brighton and District Mortuary, Lewes Road, Brighton. Wednesday 17th February 2010. 1.30. p.m.

How's the bad cold Mossy?' said Reynard as he approached Doctor Moss.

'Christ! I never heard you come in Foxy. It's alright, well nearly alright.'

'Are you sure it wasn't a hangover, you weren't half knocking 'em back on Monday.'

'It was 'knocking 'em back', as you call it, which cured me. Believe me; I'm a doctor. Hot whisky, sugar, lemon, and cloves, never fails.'

'No Mossy, *you* believe *me*.' said Reynard, 'Whisky gives you hangovers.'

'Oh shut up … what do you want?'

'It's about the girl being pregnant.'

'Yeah, I'm sorry about that. I should have seen it, but I wasn't really up to …'

'Can I ask you something?'

'About the pregnancy? Oh I know … you want to know if the foetus was alive when she was found? Well now we know the time of death and time of discovery I can assure you it wasn't.'

'Hmm, in an odd way I'm glad. But it was actually something else I want to know. Is there any way you can tell if the DNA of the foetus matches the DNA of the bit of skin Doctor Vladic found under the girl's finger nail. It's obviously scientifically possible but would such a test be legal, would the evidence stand up in court?'

'Crikey, what a question. Simple answer is, Foxy, I don't know. I can't see there'll be any problems testing the tiny bit of skin Vladic found, or indeed taking a sample of the mother's DNA, after all we've already been invasive doing the autopsy. But to do one on the foetus on which we've done *no* autopsy, we might need a court order. I'll have to check with a legal expert. How're you getting on with the investigation?'

'It's getting bigger and bigger as more suspects crop up. I'm off to see one now and I'm in a bit of a rush. Tell you what, I'll nip in tomorrow and bring you up to date. Try and have an answer on this DNA thing for me by then.'

'I'll do my best.' said Moss.

The Feathers Hotel,
10 - 24 Trafalgar Terrace, Brighton, Sussex
Wednesday 17th February 2010 2.15. p.m.

Reynard and Groves pushed the rotating glass entrance door and went into the foyer. It was huge and impressive and dominated by four tall white Corinthian pillars holding up an ornate ceiling dome. The sense of luxury and grandeur was amazing, and as they walked across the black and white marble tiles Groves couldn't help commenting on it. 'Wow … have you ever been here before, Guv?'

'Once or twice at functions, and always in the evening; I've not been here during the day.'

There was only one person on the guests' side of the white marble reception desk, she was talking to a smartly dressed young female hotel employee wearing a black suit and a manufactured smile. As Reynard and Groves approached, the guest moved off towards the lift and the receptionist turned her attention to them. 'Good afternoon Sir, Madam.' she said, adjusting the smile when she saw they had no luggage. 'Can I help you?'

Reynard responded with a smile even less genuine that hers had been while Groves, amused by the whole pantomime, put her hand over her mouth and quietly exploded. 'Yes,' he said, 'I'm here to see the manager.'

'Do you have an appointment?'

'No,' Reynard replied, taking out his warrant car and showing it to her. 'Tell him Detective Chief Inspector Reynard and Sergeant Groves are here to talk to him.'

'One moment please, I'll see if he's free.' she replied, punching a number into her desk 'phone. Almost immediately they heard ringing coming through the open door of the room immediately behind her. 'A lady and gentleman here to see you Mr Scott-Diggens,' she said, 'they're from the police.'

A moment later a short smartly dressed man came bustling out of the room and walked over to them.

'Crikey Guv … it's Poirot.' whispered Groves.

'Are you looking for me?' asked the manager. 'I haven't much time, could you come back?'

Reynard shook his head. 'It's urgent.' he said.

'Very well then you'd better come through.' the manager answered, pointing to a gap in the counter. 'I'll give you five minutes.'

Reynard, not half as relaxed as his expression indicated, nodded. 'Come on Sergeant,' he whispered 'let's humour this pompous little twit.'

When they were in his office the manager closed the door behind them, waved them to the two chairs standing in front of his desk, and took a business card from his wallet.

'Michael Scott-Diggens,' he said, passing it Reynard and pointedly looking, first at his watch, then the clock on the wall. 'Will this take long … only I've …?'

'Mr Diggens it'll …'

'It's Scott - Diggens, if you don't mind.'

'Is it?' answered Reynard, sitting motionless as a flush of annoyance crept up his throat - a bad sign which was then, as usual, followed by total and un-nerving silence.

Groves sat silent too, her hands clasped together resting on her lap.

Scott-Diggens adjusted the knot of his black tie and drew it up even tighter into the stiff collar of his pristine white shirt and then began to brush imaginary dust particles from his black jacket and pin striped trousers.

'She's right.' thought Reynard, 'he's a dead ringer for David Suchet when he's playing Poirot.'

Scott Diggens started to fidget with a pencil on his desk, first placing it on one side of the old fashioned blotter precisely parallel to its edge; then picking it up again and putting it down in the same way on the other side. Finally he looked at his watch again and tapped it.

'It's Detective *Chief* Inspector, if you don't mind.' said Reynard

'Alright Chief Inspector, I apologise. I'm sorry. Let's start again.' said Scott Diggens, 'I'm under a lot of stress.'

'And you'll be under a lot more stress sonny if your chef's arrested for murder.' thought Reynard, putting his first question. 'Do you employ a man in this hotel called Dimitri Epicurus?'

'No not quite Inspector, you have the names confused. Our restaurant is called The Epicurus Room after the Greek Philosopher of that name who advocated a life of contentment. Dimitri Papagos is our chef.'

'Hmm yes, I see.' said Reynard, hoping Groves wouldn't expose his misunderstanding of the names.

'It's about his girlfriend isn't it?' said Scott-Diggens. 'My receptionist was just telling me it was on the news last night. She's dead isn't she, murdered?'

'Had Mr Papagos not already told you?'

'No, I assume he didn't know. One lives a strange sort of life in a hotel Chief Inspector, very introspective. I often think how like it is to a closed religious community. There are some weeks during which I never put a foot out of the place; I expect he's the same. I generally meet with him in the afternoon … well … about now actually when the dining room closes after lunch. We have a coffee or a cup of tea together in the restaurant, and talk over the various issues … you know the sort of thing, I'd be there now if you hadn't come. He'll be wondering where I am.'

'Which why you you've been so restless?' said Groves, seeing Scott-Diggens in a different light.

'Yes, sorry. But he can be extremely bad tempered if he gets upset, and he's been upset since Sunday. He was like a bear with a sore head all day Monday. I was worried the way he was shouting at the staff would upset the customers. And yesterday it was worse, he turned on me. I told him if he didn't cool down he'd explode. When I left him he was brooding. They're all the same these artists … and he *is* one … good chefs *are* artists.'

As he spoke, the telephone rang. Scott- Diggens picked it up 'It's him' he mouthed to Reynard, before answering 'Yes. I'll be there in ten minutes,' he said, 'I have someone with me.'

Reynard, waited until he'd put the 'phone down again and then asked if Papagos was a good employee.

'Ah, that's the thing,' replied Scott-Diggens. 'He's not actually an employee, he's the leaseholder. He runs The Epicurus Room independently.

'Ah, does he?'

Scott-Diggens leaned forward, his elbows on his desk, his fingers steepled. 'It's like this you see Inspector, Dimitri Papagos is a Master Chef. He trained here originally under his predecessor Henri Morvaux, a man my father employed, and who was with us for his whole working life. When Henri retired, three years ago, Papagos …'

'Wait a minute … you own the hotel?'

'Third generation. My grandfather built it.'

'Right, go on.'

'Where was I ... yes … Papagos. Well he left us after he'd qualified and subsequently worked in several restaurants, mostly in London, though he did spend quite a while in Geneva and Nice. Anyway, he was working back in London when heard Henri was retiring, and he came to me with a proposition.'

'To lease the restaurant from you?'

'I knew we had to do something different even before Henri left. The hospitality industry is very competitive these days and one has to do something different to the rest if one is to succeed. Dimitri's proposition ticked all the boxes; I got rid of a loss making business which hadn't moved with the times, and replaced it with a steady income by leasing it to Dimitri. In addition, by creating a new and exciting place to eat in Brighton, we not only improved our hotel bookings we attracted a clientele we'd never had before - people who lived up to twenty miles away who were seeking somewhere more or less local where they could enjoy Michelin standard food.'

'A successful partnership then; how do you get on with Papagos personally?'

'This is confidential isn't it? I mean …'

'Everything we hear goes no further unless …'

'Unless what? I can't be frank with you if …'

'Unless it's evidence which comes up in court. But an opinion, such as the one we are hoping to secure from you will only be used to build a picture of the man in whom we are interested, and in any event will be balanced by other opinions we collect as the investigation proceeds. So, back to Mr Papagos Sir; how do you get on with him personally?'

'With difficulty.'

'You'll have to explain.'

'Will I?' said Scott-Diggens, rocking back in his chair and looking at the ceiling. 'Alright … he's a touchy opinionated bully with a ferocious temper. If I was starting again it wouldn't be with him. Is that frank enough for you, Inspector?'

'He sounds like the boss I had in my first job. It was because of him I joined the Police.'

'Yes, well I'm not sure *I'd* want to go that far.'

'So you don't think much of your lessee, right?'

'We try to keep our opinions of each other to ourselves Inspector; it's in both our interests to do so. Provided we tread carefully, keep at arm's length, and mind our own business, we manage somehow.'

'What do you know of his relationship with Roz Sommerton? asked Groves.

'Explosive!'

'Really?'

'I shouldn't have said that; better you ask him himself.'

'We're going to, but it'd be helpful if you'd give us an inkling of how you viewed their relationship, after all this is a murder enquiry.'

'Well don't tell him I told you. Their relationship was a strange one as far as I could make out; she appeared to do all the pursuing which I thought odd.'

'What does he look like?'

Surprised by her question Scott-Diggens paused for a moment. 'Look like? You mean physically, his appearance?

'Yes … is he tall dark and handsome or what?'

'I suppose women might think him good looking; he's a hulk of a man with black curly hair. You'll see what I mean soon enough if you go down to talk to him.'

'Will I? said Groves, who sensed the comments were addressed to her

Reynard, anxious to press on began to rub his knees. 'And when did you last see her, Mr Scott-Diggens?' he asked.

'On Sunday - early in the evening. She waved at me as she raced past.'

'Raced past? Where was she going?'

'Into The Epicurus Room to see Dimitri I expect. That's what I thought anyway, but she came back very soon afterwards and she was livid *and* in tears. This time she ignored me even though she nearly knocked me over. She shot out through the revolving door and disappeared down the steps. I went over to be sure she hadn't fallen or slipped … the snow you know.'

'And had she?'

'No she was arm in arm with a man I'd never seen before; they walked down to what I assumed was his car and drove off.'

'Big car was it?

'Big? I don't know … all I saw were its rear lights as it disappeared along the sea front.'

'And you never set eyes on her again?'

'No.'

'Did you ask Papagos what had happened?'

'What, and get my nose punched … I did not.'

'Hmm.' said Reynard, involuntarily touching his own nose as if he were checking it was still there. 'I think perhaps it's time for us to go and talk to Mr Papagos. Thank you for all your help Sir we may come back to you if we need more, and in the meantime don't worry, what you've told us will not be revealed anyone outside the investigation.'

As they walked back through the foyer and into The Epicurus Room they were both deep in thought. The enormous amount of background they'd just picked up pointed to the relationship between Roz Sommerton and Dimitri Papagos being mercurial.

A waiter had just put a freshly laundered cloth on a table and was laying out cutlery on it. Two tables away a woman wearing a white overall was vacuuming the carpet.

'Where do we find Mr Papagos? asked Reynard.

The waiter nodded in the direction of a pair of double doors partially hidden by a large screen covered with tapestry. 'Through there.'

They walked across the room and into the kitchen, trying to imagine at which table the McWilliams were about to sit when Roz came 'flying' past. A boy was cleaning down a stainless steel top immediately inside the door. He must have been nearly finished for all the rest of the dozen or so they could see were bright and shining like the rows of pans lined up on the shelves beneath them. Right at the back of the room, and pinning a piece of paper to a cork covered board fixed to the wall behind his desk, was a burly man with black curly hair. He was wearing chef's whites and had a red and white spotted bandana tied round his head. It had to be Papagos. He turned when he heard their step. 'You can't come in here.'

Reynard responded by showing his warrant card, as did Groves. 'Police.' he said.

Papagos swivelled his high backed office chair round and sat on it, his face slumping as quickly as had his body, his olive-coloured skin going paler by the second. 'Oh Christ!'

'We want to have word with you about …'

'About Roz … yes ... I knew you'd come.'

'Where can we talk?' asked Reynard. 'this isn't a good place … somewhere more private.'

Papagos nodded. 'Restaurant.' he said.

They went back single file into The Epicurus Room, where Papagos dismissed the waiter and the cleaner and conducted them to a circular table in one corner. Groves slid round the banquette seat, leaving the two arm chairs for the men. Papagos bent forward, rested his folded arms on the table and lay his forehead on them. 'I knew you'd come,' he mumbled into his sleeves. 'I didn't do it. I didn't kill Roz. I had a row with her, yes, I tried to shake sense into her and in the end, God forgive me, I hit her. But I didn't kill her … and I've not been to Fyling Castle since I was a kid. You've got to believe me; it's not me you want.'

Reynard paused and then said: 'This is likely to take a while Mr Papagos, do you want some water or anything before we start?'

Papagos raised his head and turned to look at Reynard, his complexion already on its way back to his normal Mediterranean tan. 'No nothing, get on with it … I didn't do it. When one of the porters came over to me yesterday and said he was sorry to hear about Roz I thought he meant he was sorry we'd fallen out - everyone in the kitchen heard the row we had on Sunday night. I had no idea he meant he was sorry she was dead. I told him to mind his own bloody business and get on with his work; they must have all heard what I said to him as well so nobody opened their mouth after that. I didn't discover Roz was dead until this morning when a guy delivering vegetables *also* said how sorry he was. I asked him what the hell he was talking about and he told me.'

'It was in all the papers.' said Reynard,

'I never read a paper.'

'It was on the television as well.' said Groves.

'I hardly ever watch television and I seldom leave the building. I'm either down here working my arse off, or upstairs in my room fast asleep. You've no idea how tiring this job can be with that fat little bastard looking for your blood every month.'

'What 'fat little bastard' - Mr Scott-Diggens?'

'Who else? He conned me into leasing this place with his fancy computer figures. It was only when I got it up and running I saw he'd shoved the targets up too fucking high. If it hadn't have been for Roz stepping in I'd have been out on my neck by now. I suppose you could say it's what eventually led to the problems I had with her.'

Reynard held up his hand 'Hang on Mr Papagos, you're going far too fast for me. Go back a bit. What did you mean when you say targets?'

'Covers for lunch, and covers for dinner.'

'He fixes the number of tablecloths you use - you're kidding me?'

'Christ no … no, no, no. Covers are people, the number of covers we did just now was thirty one, in other words thirty one people came for lunch. It's a measure of how busy we've been and whether we're likely to have been profitable. I have a certain minimum target I must achieve each day for lunch and dinner. He gets a small percentage on my takings and all the profit the wine cellar and bars make from people who eat here; the more people I get in the more money he makes.'

'Yes … and …?'

'And if I don't hit the targets, which I can now see have been too high from the start, the rent I pay for the lease goes up because I have to pay a penalty.'

'But didn't you agree all this before you signed it up to it, you must have done?'

'Of course I did, but it's going to take two more years to get up to the target he set. Some weeks I miss it by miles and when that happens he's down on me like a ton of bricks, wielding the penalty clause.'

'You'll have to explain.'

'If my covers fall below target his bar profits do too, and to compensate him I have to give him an increased percentage of my turnover.'

'So he wins no matter what?'

'Unless I go belly-up yes … the bastard. He conned me I told you. Ah it might go alright in the end but for the next year or two I'm going to have problems in some weeks.'

'And if you can't find the cash to pay the penalties you're in more trouble, yes I see.'

'Exactly. Problem is my money's tied up in repayments for all extra equipment I had to buy, so with no funds to cover the payments he demands my debt to him keeps rising.'

Groves, who'd been listening and taking notes, saw the connection before he came to it. 'And your girlfriend Roz, stepped in with the extra funds and saved the day.' she said. 'She paid him, on your behalf?'

'Yes, but I always said it was a loan.'

'Some loan - twenty two thousand pounds.'

'How did you know how much it was?'

'Mr Papagos we're conducting a murder enquiry - we've been through Roz Sommerton's papers. You say you always considered it a loan?'

'I wish I'd never agreed to it at all. I'd have been better if I'd chucked it in and starting again somewhere else. It's been nothing but trouble from the word 'Go'. First from him, then from her.'

Groves shuffled in her seat as cramp bit into her leg; she tried rubbing it but in the end she had to get up and pace about. 'Sorry Sir, cramp.'

Reynard nodded and went back to Papagos. 'What sort of trouble did you get from her then?'

'Deceit for a start.'

'Really? Regarding what?'

'Her intentions.'

'Explain … I don't understand.'

Groves sat down again, a smile on her face. 'I think I do.' she said, 'Roz wanted to be recompensed for stepping in … am I right?'

Papagos nodded, and gave a sheepish grin in response. 'It's stupid, and I don't quite know how to put it without appearing to be … well …'

'Vain?'

'I suppose so.'

'She wanted to advance your relationship?'

'Yes.'

'But you didn't. She fancied you but you weren't too pushed about her, am I right?'

'Sort of … yes. I only got to know her when she was in here doing an article on the best places to eat in Brighton. I suppose I turned it on a bit to get the right side of her. If I knew then what I know now I'd have stayed clear of her, a long way clear of her.'

Reynard suddenly seemed to have worked out was going on as well, and started tapping his chin. 'She was in love with you, yes? But you didn't feel the same about her … now I see the problem.'

But Sergeant Groves shook her head. 'I don't think that's quite what Mr Papagos meant when he said she *fancied* him. It was all about sex wasn't it Mr Papagos?'

'I think I will have a drink of water,' he replied, 'I'll get it, Anyone else?'

'I can see bottles of Malvern water over there on a sideboard.' said Reynard, 'Would you mind Sergeant.'

Groves got up and went for the water giving Reynard the opportunity to cross-examine Papagos more closely.

'So what was the row actually about?'

'Ah Inspector I feel so stupid telling you.'

'You're not the first to be bamboozled by a woman son, get it off your chest … what happened?'

'OK, but don't tell her.'

'Who Sergeant Groves … alright … but hurry up she'll be back soon.'

'She tricked me.'

'Who Sergeant Groves?'

'No Roz; I thought she was doing me a favour lending me the money, but what she actually wanted was to get me into her bed.'

'And did you … 'er … get into her bed?'

'She's a very attractive women inspector … not my type but a terrific looker. Well, I thought … she's done me a favour

… if this is what she wants in the way of a 'thank you'… why not; it wasn't going to cost me anything. Little did I know.'

'I don't understand.'

'When I seemed to hesitate she misunderstood me. 'Don't worry,' she said, 'I'm on the pill.'

'And you … 'er … obliged.'

'I did, but she'd been lying, and that's what caused the row on Sunday. She'd not been on the pill at all and she came in on Sunday to tell me she was pregnant. Pleased as anything she was.'

'You hit the roof of course and refused to take responsibility for her or the baby.'

'No, no, no you've got it wrong, I would have looked after her *and* the baby; what sort of a man d'you think I am? Of course I would, but I didn't get a chance because she ditched me. Right there in front of all my staff … gave me the bullet and asked for her twenty two thousand back … the money she'd always insisted was a gift. Oh …I … I …'

'Could have killed her?'

'Water?' said Groves putting a tray with three glasses and three bottles on the table.

'Not for me, Sergeant. I want to move on a bit to clarify something first. Where were you on Sunday night Mr Papagos between the hours if six and ten?'

Papagos laughed. 'Here of course, where else? Sunday's our second most busy night, and last Sunday was especially so - fifty one covers - well over target. You'll find plenty of people who'll tell you I was here from about four in the afternoon until two in the morning or later.'

'You didn't nip out for an hour or so?'

'Not a chance.'

'What sort of car have you got?'

'What … I don't have one.'

'Who's Geoff?'

'Not a clue … Geoff? I don't know any Geoffs. Who *is* he?'

'Who's the Irishman she's been seeing lately?'

'D'you mean her uncle?'

'No I did not mean her uncle … at least I don't think I did. I didn't know she had an uncle.'

'Oh yes, he turned up out of the blue recently. He's her mother's … no wait a minute … her father's brother.

'Do you know how we can find this 'uncle' of hers … we'll have to talk to him?'

'Well it shouldn't be too hard,' said Papagos, 'he's one of your lot.'

Reynard, who was about to get up to leave promptly sat down again. What d'you mean - our lot?'

'What d'you think?'

'Someone in the Police Force?'

'It's what she told me.' said Papagos.

Reynard paused for moment trying to make up his mine what to do next and then when he had, he made a second attempt to rise. 'It's back to the office for us I think Sergeant, we've a spot of research to do. In the meantime don't leave the town without telling us Mr Papagos, and thank you for being so frank.'

As they walked out of the hotel Reynard began to laugh.

'Blimey, Guv,' said Groves, 'What's so funny - I wouldn't have thought we had much to laugh at.'

'It's not laughter.' he said, 'It's 'shock and awe' isn't that what they say. We've Irishmen, Englishmen and Greeks; we've chefs, policemen and soldiers; we've Geoffs and 'Chefs' and Herberts and Dimitris; God Almighty … what haven't we got?

'We haven't got a decent suspect, that's what we haven't got.' said Groves, 'So what'll we do now?'

'What indeed? For a start we'll button our lips; we'll tell the Super he might have a murderer in the camp, and we'll stop at the pub over there and kill a Famous Grouse or two. Got a better idea? No? Good. Let's go.'

Sussex Police Major Incident Suite,
Sussex House, Brighton Sussex.
Wednesday 17th February 2010. 4.50 p.m.

The rest of the Roz Sommerton murder investigation team were sitting patiently in Chief Inspector Reynard's office waiting for him so they could set out what was to be done the next day. He was in with Superintendent Bradshaw, giving him details of the interviews he'd had with Scott-Diggens and Papagos in The Feathers Hotel, and had just wound up by repeating Papagos's astonishing revelation.

'I don't believe it.' said the Super. 'One of our people the murderer of your victim. Rubbish. Murdered a pint, yes; but murder Roz Sommerton, never.'

'Groves and I feel the same but we have to allow for the fact it might be true and act accordingly.'

'It'll mean handing the case over to another constabulary - Hampshire or Surry say, maybe even Kent.'

'I realise that Sir, but what else can we do?'

'Are you sure it wasn't just a ruse to put us off?'

'No I'm not … it may eventually turn out to be one, but how can we tell? I suggest we work on the remote chance it is true and see what we can discover.'

'Right. Make sure Groves says nothing, and tell the other two something sensitive's come up and the case has been put on hold. In fact you can send Furness back to Shoreham.'

'Right Sir, I'll talk to them. What'll I do then?'

'Don't tempt me!'

'No, seriously Sir, once I know Groves and Best and Furness are out of the way I'll hang around here until I hear from you, shall I? I've a bit of research on a legal and medical issue regarding a DNA test to do anyway; I've plenty to keep me occupied.'

'Good. I'll ring you as soon as I've spoken to the Chief Constable and something's been set up. Now, go and inform your team and then go home and talk to Cathy for a change.'

'If it's all the same to you Sir I'd like to call in see Doctor Moss on the way home. Whoever ultimately winds up with the case will still need to resolve this legal and medical issue which concerns taking a DNA sample from the foetus of Roz's baby. After I've spoken to him I'll go home. Tomorrow I'll come in and stay in my office until you contact me.'

'Alright, I'll call you at home tonight if anything breaks. Now go and sort out your team Foxy and once they're gone, go yourself.'

'Thank you Sir, we anticipated we'd be taken off the case as soon as Papagos told us about Roz's uncle having a Police connection so we've prepared a story already.'

'Ah … and what is it?'

'Well, it's as close to the truth as we can get.'

'Without raising suspicion?'

'Of course; I'm going to tell them what Sergeant Groves and I agreed earlier - we've been temporarily stood down because we've inadvertently stumbled into a 'sting' operation being undertaken by another division, and we've to back off until the priorities are ironed out by the Chief Constable.'

'Sounds plausible. OK, let's hope it sticks.'

'Groves is going to take all the paperwork we've collected home and go through it again. She'll stay there until I send for her which, if you can get a speedy agreement on how the case is to be handled, could be what … some-time tomorrow or the day after? I'll ask Best to switch his attention to the PharmoChem drugs theft enquiry which we haven't touched this week, and I'll send Furness back to Shoreham to re-interview the woman who complained of being raped and then to continue chasing information on the cars he's already looking into.'

'And you'll be here … but why? It'd be an opportunity for you to take a couple of days leave; you never seem to use your entitlement.'

'Because Sir, if I did so I'm likely to find myself wallpapering the flamin' dining room!'

'Oh right, yes, good enough … well go and hide somewhere.'

'I will, and I'll be expecting your call.'

'Fine …now go and talk to the troops.'

***

'Change of plan.' said Reynard, closing the door behind him and making for his chair. 'It seems we've blundered into a sting being conducted by the drugs squad.'

'You're joking.' said Best.

Reynard glared at him. 'I am not joking Constable, thank you. And I am not happy the murder we're investigating is now to take second place to a lousy hunt for quarter of a ton of flaming Ecstasy tablets. But I *am* under orders to stand down and there's nothing I can do about it. We're to hold our hand on the Roz Sommerton case until further notice.'

Best's anger was as evident Reynard's had seemed. 'And possibly allow her killer to get away.' he said, 'Jesus that's criminal, especially as we were just getting to grips with things.'

'It's no good protesting I've tried. Now here's what we're going to do and please … please … do as I ask.'

'I suppose I'll have to go back to Shoreham.' said Furness.

'In a way you will, yes.' Reynard replied. 'I've secured permission for you to continue with two elements of our case provided you work from home and keep in touch with me by 'phone only. You are not to come to this office. Understand?'

'Yes, but what am I to do?'

'Have another talk with the woman who's accusing McCloskey, prod her a bit, and see if you can find out what he really did to her. Maybe it'd be a good idea if Sergeant Groves accompanied you. What d'you think Sergeant?'

'OK by me Guv,' she answered, 'I don't want to be stuck here twiddling my thumbs. D.C. Furness can call me on my mobile when he's got an appointment to see this woman. We can liaise by telephone, no need to come in here at all.'

'And what was the second thing … 'er … Guv?' asked Furness still apprehensive about addressing the D.C.I. in such familiar terms.'

'Keep trying to track down the cars.'

'What'll I do Guv?' asked Best.

'You can try and get some movement into the PharmoChem theft. We've tended to concentrate on the fraud angle because the accounts looked fishy but maybe there's something else. I want you to read all the files and write down what you make of them. Sergeant Groves has them at the moment.'

'Where will we find you if we need to ask you anything Guv?' asked Best. 'And how long d'you think the Sommerton case will be held up.'

'If I knew that Constable I'd be a Chief Superintendent, not a Chief Inspector. Now off with you all, I've things to do. I'll telephone you as soon as I have news.'

As he walked along the line of cars to get to his own, an upstairs window opened above him and Sergeant Crowther stuck his head out. 'Trying to avoid me are you, you crafty sod?'

Reynard gave him a dismissive wave with his hand and took his car key from his pocket.

'You owe me ten quid.' shouted Crowther.

'Reynard poised with the car door half open, looked up. 'What for?'

'My body's just turned up so unless you've got someone in handcuffs stashed away, I win.'

Reynard waved again, got into his car and drove off mumbling 'Stuff you mate.'

Brighton and District Mortuary, Lewes Road, Brighton. Wednesday 17th February 2010. 5.30. p.m.

Doctor Vladic was sitting at his desk filling in a form. 'Cursed things.' he said to Reynard when he saw him coming through the door. 'It takes me longer to complete the damned documentation than it does to do the post mortem … and it's getting worse.'

'Tell me about it.' Reynard replied, 'Is …?'

'No he left about an hour ago. I think he's gone to talk to a solicitor pal of his … something to do with DNA sampling. I believe it's connected to your case.'

'Oh right … never mind I'll see him tomorrow.'

'No you won't he's not coming in tomorrow, he's going up to London. I think it's to do with your case as well.'

'Is it? Who's he calling on.'

'He said needed to check something with the legal department in the BMC, so I suppose that's where he's going.'

'The British Medical Council eh? I'll have to wait until he gets back then.'

'It's what he said.'

'OK, tell him I was in when you next see him.'

'Sure.' said Vladic, picking up his pen and returning to his form-filling.

14, Malvern Gardens, Brighton, Sussex. Wednesday 17th February 2010. 5.55. p.m

Reynard's wife was sitting on the sofa waiting for the news to start when he walked in. 'Glory be,' she said. 'what's happened? The supper's nowhere near ready.'

'Problem.'

'I'll switch the oven on; it'll be an hour, I've a treat for you tonight - one of your favourites - steak and kidney pie. What's the problem?'

Reynard tapped his nose then put his finger across his lips. 'Confidential.' he said, in not much above a whisper.

'Come on Foxy, who am *I* going to tell?

'No one … I know … but I just want to make sure; this case is going to blow up any minute.'

'Roz Sommerton's murder?'

'Yes. I've had a tip off someone in the job's involved. Bradshaw went bananas when I told him and he's taken me off the case. In fact he's put a complete stopper on the investigation until he talks to the C.C.'

'That'll be alright you get on well with him don't you, especially after his pal Nelson Deep was murdered last year and you found out who did it.'

'It won't make any difference, I'll be off the case for sure, 'Prunes' will hand it over to another county, he has to.'

'And you've been sent home like a naughty schoolboy.'

'There's not much I can do about it, we have to use officers who are detached from the person under investigation.'

'Who is it? I won't tell anyone.'

'I haven't the faintest idea that's what's so daft. But it could be any one of the thirty people who work in Sussex House, from the Super down to the cleaner.'

'So what happens now? What do *you* do?'

'Ah this is all new to me Cathy, I haven't a clue. If I was to guess though, the Super'll have me hovering in the background waiting to take over again if this new man, this uncle of Roz's, who's said to be 'one of us', gets eliminated. Furthermore, I'm sure to be asked to brief the team the C.C. calls in. It's even conceivable I'll be allowed to keep working on other men we've identified who are known to have connections to Roz, but not to the police.'

'How long will they keep you dangling?'

'Again I have no idea, because it's not happened to me before. But at a guess, it'll all be sorted by this time tomorrow.'

'Let's have a drink.'

'Good idea; I could do with one ... what d'you want?'

'G&T.'

'Right, and I'll have a Famous Grouse.'

As Cathy Reynard went out to turn on the oven Foxy made for the drinks cabinet. It was the second time in a week he'd been home early and they had a quiet evening in front of the television once they'd eaten, purposely avoiding discussing the case. It didn't stop them thinking though, and each of them spent the entire evening going through everyone they knew who worked in Sussex House, trying to guess which of them might be Roz Sommerton's uncle, and possibly her killer.

Thursday 18th February

14, Malvern Gardens, Brighton, Sussex. Thursday 18th February 2010. 7.30 a.m.

Cathy was still asleep when Foxy got back up to their bedroom with a tray on which he'd laid out her breakfast of orange juice, tea, two slices of buttered toast, and a pot of marmalade. She stirred and sat up as he put the tray down on the bedside table.

'What's happened?' she asked, practically overwhelmed by the shock of being served her breakfast in bed. 'I thought we were going to have lazy morning.'

'So did I,' he replied, 'but I still woke at six despite the Famous Grouse.'

'Are you not having any breakfast?'

'Had it downstairs an hour ago; I'm ready for Hobnob and a cup of coffee now, and I can't understand why 'his Nibs' hasn't rung. '

'Colin Bradshaw?'

'Yes he was going to speak to the C.C last night, and I was sure he'd be on to me first thing this morning to fill me in.'

'Well if you're going to be on edge all day why don't *you* ring *him*?'

'D'you think I should?'

'I don't think you should, but I wish you would. You'll have me driven crackers if you hang around here all day pacing about like a caged lion waiting for his dinner.'

'I'll have shower and get dressed. If he hasn't rung by then, I'll ring him. Fair enough?'

'Fair enough Foxy, you go and do whatever you have to do while I enjoy my treat.' she said, buttering a piece of toast and reaching for the marmalade.

Half an hour later and down in the kitchen again, he was about to make a jug of coffee when in the distance he heard the muffled ring tone of his mobile 'phone. He dashed through into the hall, patted his overcoat pockets until he found it, and then yanked it out. 'Damnation, too late.' he said, when there was no one at the other end.

As he walked back to the kitchen to make the coffee a 'message received' ping came from the 'phone in his hand. He checked it - four missed calls and an unread text message.

'Christ Almighty, they're all at it except me!' he said, responding to the information on the telephone screen by taking a seat at the kitchen table and tapping the numbers on the keypad as instructed.

The first voice-mail message he played had been the last one received; it must have been the one he'd just missed. It was from the Superintendent: 'Message received at eight-o-five a.m., today. 'It's Colin Bradshaw, Foxy. Call me as soon as you get this message. I drove up and saw the C.C. last night at his home. He telephoned a few people while I was with him and told me he'd ring me sometime this morning. He's just done so to say a senior officer from the Surrey Constabulary, D.C.S. Charles Le Saux, that's L E ... S A U X, is on his way down from Guildford to take the investigation over at least until the conflict of interest re this 'Irish Uncle' is sorted. Once everything's regarding him is clarified he'll either continue, or hand it back to you. Ring me ASAP.'

He looked at his watch 'It's too early to call him yet. I'll try after nine, and in the meantime … coffee.' He went over, switched on the Cona Coffee machine and called up the second message. It was from Doctor Moss. 'Message received at seven forty four a.m., today. 'It's Mossy. I'm on my way to London Foxy, and when I get back some time after lunch will you spare me a few minutes for a chat. I can see you in your office or you can call round to mine. I'll ring you when I'm within half an hour of Brighton, OK?'

'Let's hope you get the answer we want my friend.' Reynard said under his breath. 'We're going damned well backwards at the moment … what we need is a boost. Getting the foetus's DNA and tying it to the skin under Roz's nail will go some way towards doing that, especially if we get a sample from Dimitri and find his claim to be the father is correct.'

'What are you mumbling on about?' said Cathy who, unheard by him, had come downstairs and into the kitchen with the milk jug in her hand.'

'Ah … it's about a DNA sample we're having a problem with. Why the jug?'

'You didn't put anything in it, you lemon!'

'Oh sorry … give it me I'll fill it.'

'No Foxy, I'll fill it. You can get on with your worrying.'

The third voice mail was from Sergeant Jack Crowther. 'Message received at eight-o-two a.m., today. 'It's Jack Crowther. Where the hell are you, Foxy? Call me as soon as you get this.'

'If he's looking for his money, he can wait.' said Reynard, bringing forward the final piece of voice mail. It was from Sergeant Groves. 'Message received at seven twenty nine a.m., today. 'Morning Guv, I'm sure you're up and about like me. I might have had a bit of luck yesterday evening when I was going through Roz's stuff and came across the entry in her desk diary which said 'Book Beeches and Willows'. If you recollect, at the time we found it and the one on the twentieth of August saying 'Remind Mum to be around', I speculated on her being pregnant. Well now we know she was pregnant, I chanced finding a connection between 'Beech' and 'Willows' and babies. It wasn't hard to find one: Doctor Eamon Beech is a gynaecologist and obstetrician in Worthing and The Willows is the private Nursing Home, also in Worthing where he sends many of his patients. I rang his secretary late yesterday afternoon and she confirmed Rosaleen Sommerton is one of them. I'd have rung you last night but decided not to spoil your evening. Anything new from the Super? Ring me when you have some; I hate being side-lined like this.'

'Me too.' thought Reynard, bringing up the text message which had been sent the previous evening. It was from Furness. 'Found McCloskey/Sommerton car at International Car Auctions, Southampton. He bought a banger for four hundred same auction Tuesday a.m. and took cash balance of two thousand two hundred. Checked ferries. He sailed Cherbourg ex Southampton yesterday taking the banger with him. I have car details. Must have arrived Cherbourg early this morning and could be half way across France by now. Do you want me check with French Police?'

'Hmm,' said Reynard, noting the 'bumping' of boiling water in one of the Cona jugs and getting up and pouring it through the pyramid of coffee in the funnel over the other one, 'this fella Furness is bright; Best'll have to watch his step.'

As soon as the coffee had filtered through he poured himself a cup and took it, the phone, and the notes he'd made, into the sitting room where he pulled back the curtains. Outside the sun had just risen and the night's fresh fall of snow was taking on a pink glow.'

'Nice from in here,' he said, making for his armchair 'but I bet it's damned cold outside.'

He'd hardly sat down when he heard the clatter of the letterbox. 'Ah - the paper.'

He got up and went into the hall where their copy of The Globe was lying on the front door mat. Roz Sommerton's picture was on the front page. Over it, the caption said: 'Globe's investigative journalist murdered', while underneath in a short speculative and much hackneyed phrase the reader was told: 'Police confident of early arrest.' It brought the first smile of the day to Reynard's face.

The unattributed piece which followed mainly dealt with the achievements Roz had attained since joining the paper and went on to suggest her death may have come as a result of one of her fearless and critical appraisals.

'They could be right,' he thought, 'but I don't think they are. The fact she was a self-opinionated grasping bully who preyed on men and took them for all she could get is a much more likely reason for her being killed than the fact she shot verbal arrows at a few people. And now this irritating complication regarding her uncle has cropped up and it's likely to deprive me of the satisfaction of sorting out the facts and putting the story together.'

He felt sick he was so frustrated. The clock on the mantle-piece striking nine brought him back to earth though, and he reached for his coffee. It was cold. He was just about to go and get fresh one before ringing the Super when his mobile started to ring. 'Oh God … it'll be him.' It was.

'Did you not get the message I sent earlier?'

'Yes Sir, I did. I was leaving it until nine; I know how many are queuing up to see you first thing.'

'Yes, well … The point is Le Saux, do you know him by the way?'

'No Sir, I've heard of him of course.'

'As he has of you. Anyway he'll be here at two to two thirty, and I want you here when he arrives.'

'Not a problem Sir, I'll be there. Has anyone been looking for me?'

'I don't think so … Jack Crowther's been hovering around asking if anyone knew where you were, but he didn't ask me, and I wouldn't have told him if he had. Just make sure you're here at two.'

After the Super had rung off he telephoned Furness. 'You've done well tracking McCloskey to France, Constable; what made you think of trying the ferry companies?'

'Thank you Guv; I just put myself in his shoes. If I wanted to escape from something which was going to bring me down I'd get as much cash as I could and slip out of reach as quickly as possible. Selling my car by auction and taking a ferry to France is exactly what I'd have done myself; that's all. It's not even police work … it's guessing.'

'I hate to say it but you'd be surprised how much police work *is* guessing Constable, or perhaps I should say and '*out* guessing'; it's how we catch 'em. For the moment though we'd better leave things as they are; contacting the French is beyond our brief. Did you have any luck with the Irish car?'

'No Sir I was concentrating on McCloskey's. I'll get on to the other one this afternoon. This morning Sergeant Groves is coming over to help me re-interview McCloskey's alleged victim.'

'Fair enough, keep me in touch.'

'I'll ring or text you tonight Sir.'

He rang D.C. Best, but his mobile was switched off. 'I hope he has a good reason,' said Reynard, 'or I'll have his …'

'Have his what?' asked Cathy, by then dressed and pulling on her overcoat.

'Guts for garters … where are you going?'

'Walkies!'

'Hang on I'll come with you, I quite fancy a stroll in the snow. Where is he?'

'He' came padding in, his lead in his mouth, an elderly black and white cocker spaniel. They were gone for an hour and a half and were barely home when The William Tell Overture started to fill the air again. 'Just a minute,' cried Reynard, digging his hand into his pocket.

It was Doctor Moss; he'd just got back.

'Where are you Mossy? … Oh home … Alright … sure … why not? Where do you live?'

'I thought you said we'd go down to The Cricketers for an early lunch.' said Cathy, who'd had her fingers crossed since the phone began ringing.

'And so we will,' Reynard answered, 'I'm just going to slip over to Mossy's, he says his cold's coming back but I need the information he's got. Don't worry I'll be home in an hour.

Westwinds, Marine Road, Brighton, Sussex
Thursday 18th February 2010. 11.50.a.m.

Reynard rang the bell then turned to look across the white blanket of snow covering the golf course. In the distance he could see the criss-crossed masts of dozens of boats pulled up on 'the hard' of the town's smart new marina - a sight to promise much on a sunny day - but a strangely incongruous one in swirling snow.

Doctor Moss opened the door and, smiling weakly, stood back into the hallway to let Reynard past. 'Come on in,' he said, 'thanks for driving over … I'm not feeling all that …'

'I can see you're not. Christ man you look awful. Are you alright?'

'No I'm not,' Moss replied, taking Reynard's coat and leading him into the sitting room. 'and I'm worried to death. Come in and have a drink I need to talk to you.'

'Not for me thanks, and you shouldn't either mate you're drinking too much.'

Moss nodded dejectedly but still half-filled a cut glass tumbler with whisky from a decanter on the sideboard. 'Sit down Foxy, I have something to tell you.' he said.

Reynard took a seat in a leather tub chair and started to rub his knees. 'This isn't about your trip to London is it Mossy? It's something to do with you *personally* isn't it … you're not well.'

Moss shook his head.

'Have you been to see anyone, doctors are always the last ones to look after themselves.'

Moss wrinkled his face up as if he were in pain. 'It's not that, Foxy.' he said.

'OK, so what is it?'

'I hardly dare tell you.'

'Tell me what?'

'It's me you're looking for.'

'What're you talking about?'

'Rosaleen Sommerton was my niece. I'm her uncle Foxy. I should have told you from the beginning but once I didn't …. well … you know …'

Reynard shot up straight in the chair and clapped his hands to his head. 'You're what? But you're not even Irish.'

'I am. I was born in Tipperary. As a matter of fact …'

'No, no, stop this Mossy, you can't …'

'But I want to tell you, I should have done it from the start; you'd have understood I know you would. It was just …'

'I'm off the bloody case.'

'Oh no … since when?'

'Since yesterday when we found out there was someone in the job involved. Look Mossy I'm sorry, but you mustn't say another word to me. I'll be in a ton of trouble if I was caught talking to you, and it wouldn't do *you* much good either; think about it. Get yourself a decent 'brief' no matter what it costs you.'

'Yeah, I suppose I should.'

Reynard still visibly shaken stood up. 'Of course you should … and don't waste time doing it. God Almighty … *you* that girl's uncle … *unbelievable!*'

'I know … I'm sorry. It's a long story, you see …"

Reynard held out his hand. 'Don't … don't … I'd hear you out Mossy but I can't …I'm sure you understand.'

Moss wrinkled up his face again and nodded.

'Stay here with your mobile switched on; I'll go and talk to the Super. Does your wife know about all this?

'No not yet, she's playing golf.'

'Right … well you'd better have a word with your solicitor before she comes home.'

'What the hell am I'm going to say him - or her. She'll be furious … I've made a right mess of everything.'

Reynard lifted his eyebrows and gave a sympathetic nod then made for the front door. 'I've got to go.' he said, stepping out into the falling snow and heading down the drive to the gate. As he was about lift the latch, he glanced back. Moss was standing with one hand on the edge of the front door; the other was half-raised in a farewell salute.

14, Malvern Gardens, Brighton, Sussex.
Thursday 18th February, 2007. 12.30.pm.

'That didn't take long.' said Cathy; about to go upstairs as Foxy stepped into the hall.

'More's the pity; I thought I was going for nice quiet chat with Mossy but …'

'But he wasn't there?'

'Oh he was there alright, but what he had to tell me wasn't what I was expecting, and now I've a real problem on my hands.'

'Do you want to call off our lunch?'

'Yes … no. No … we'll have lunch; it'll give me time to think. What time do they start serving?'

'In the carvery? About now I think.'

Reynard looked at his watch 'OK it's half past. If we go immediately I'll have time to get my head round what I've just learned while we're eating. Talking it over with you might be a good way to see which way I ought to go.'

As Reynard spoke Cathy's expression became more and more perplexed. 'What on earth's happened, Foxy, you look as though you've seen a ghost?'

'I have … I'll tell you when we get there.' he said, as she stepped off the bottom stair and reached into the closet for her coat.

The Cricketers pub was practically empty as they walked through the saloon bar and into the carvery. 'Too early are we?' asked Reynard, pointedly looking up at a clock hanging on the wall over the door to the kitchen. 'No, boss, you're fine. I'm just about to put the joints out; give me two minutes and I'll be ready to serve you, I've a nice leg of lamb on today.'

'That'll do me; what about you Cathy?'

'Yes, lamb'll be fine.'

'Bit of everything to go with it? I've boiled and roast, and carrots and cabbage.' said the white hatted chef, as he set up the joint on a wooden carving block.

'Yes, fine - a bit of everything.' said Reynard, turning and grimacing at Cathy who'd taken her seat.

'Don't worry it'll be alright.' she whispered, more in hope than expectation. 'I'll have the same.'

'I wish we'd gone to the Dog and Duck.'

'They don't do food there anymore. Now come on, get it out, what happened at Mossy's?'

'You'll never believe it.'

'Try me.'

'He's the one.'

'The one what?'

'Roz's uncle.'

'The Irish uncle you were talking about?'

'Yeah. You could have knocked me down with a feather.'

'But he's not Irish.'

'He *is*.'

'No … never … you can tell.'

'And his brother was Roz's father.'

'Has he ever mentioned his family before?'

'I don't think so.'

'Go on then.'

Reynard was about to answer when the chef called out 'Ready when you are.' and walked to the till at the end of the serving counter. 'Want any desert?' he asked, his finger poised ready to punch up the bill. 'There's apple pie and ice cream.'

'No… have you anything else?' asked Reynard, walking over to collect the tray on which their lunches had been put.

The chef nodded. 'Yeah - there's ice cream and apple pie.' he said, letting out roar of laughter.

Reynard, not in the mood for joking, shook his head.

'Well?' said Cathy, when he got back to his seat. 'Go on.'

'Go on what?'

'Did Mossy ever mention his family?'

'No, not until this morning he didn't, and I left the minute he told me. He was in a hell of a state mind you … bottling it up … not telling anyone … you know. Point is where does it leave *me*?'

'It doesn't leave you anywhere, you're off the case. Why d'you think he tried to keep his relationship to her so secret?'

'I've no idea.'

'Guilt?'

'Oh Cathy come on … of course not … mind you he did act funny that first day up in the tent when Geordie Hawkins first brushed off the snow and he saw her face.'

'Look, if he *had* killed her and dumped her up there he'd found an excuse to send someone else to the scene instead, so it must mean he didn't do it.'

'If he'd sent Vladic, a relative junior, when I'd been told he was available himself, I'd have questioned him and then he'd have to say why.'

'True.'

'I suppose he knew he'd give himself away if he was pressed too hard. Maybe he thought if he had a whisky or two to stiffen himself up he'd get away with it.'

'Get away with it! You're talking as though he's guilty, and he's your friend.'

'Not if he killed someone he isn't. To tell you the truth, Cathy when I saw the amount he was drinking on Monday I knew there was something wrong. I even questioned him about it, he was at it non-stop; he could have been drinking all night trying to forget.'

'Ah no.'

'He was really knocking them back in the pub … I should have twigged.'

'Eat your lunch it'll get cold … it's not bad actually; the vegetables have still got some bite left in them.'

'I'll take your word for it.' said Reynard, pushing his food to one side.

Cathy smiled at the chef who'd seen him do it and was looking apprehensively at the leg of lamb under the heating lamps. 'It's very good … excellent,' she called over to him. 'my husband's just not hungry.'

'Would he rather have something else?'

Reynard shook his head.

'No he's alright.' Said Cathy, putting down her knife and fork and laying her hand on Foxy's. 'Stop fretting … you're off the case … it's someone else's problem now.'

Reynard growled through his clenched teeth and jabbed the air with his fist. 'That's the damned thing Cathy, I want it both ways - I don't want to be involved with anything to do with Mossy - but do want to be kept in the loop. If the Super'll wear it I'd still like to be 'in' somehow. And there's another thing … what am I going to say to the others, to Lucy and Best, and this new lad Furness, we haven't even got Roz's 'Irish Uncle' down as a suspect.'

'He'll be one now though, won't he?'

'Who Mossy? I can't believe it.'

'Look, for Goodness sake, the best way to get him back on his pedestal is to find out who really killed the poor girl.'

'I know it is, but if I'm off the case how am I going to …?'

'You might only be off as far as Mossy is concerned. As soon as he's in the clear you'll be back.'

'D'you think so … really … I don't. Anyway for the moment it's out of my hands.' Reynard answered. 'Do *you* want any apple pie and ice cream?'

Cathy didn't answer; she was trying to picture the look on Superintendent Bradshaw's face when he heard Foxy's news.

Chief Superintendent Bradshaw's office
Sussex Police Major Incident Suite,
Sussex House, Brighton Sussex.
Thursday 18th February 2010 1.46.pm

He's what?' The exclamation of surprise Superintendent Bradshaw let out could be heard all over the building.

'It was a shock to me too Sir,' said Reynard, 'though in retrospect I can see how it might explain his odd behaviour. I thought he had a really bad cold; he told me he had in fact, but now I can see it could just as easily be an excuse he adopted to keep me at a distance.'

The Superintendent, who'd hardly listened to a word Reynard had said, nodded. 'He was fooling you in other words.'

'What time are you expecting Le Saux to arrive Sir? Only if I may, I'd like to ask …'

'He's here … up in the canteen I think, that's where I sent him; he has a D.C.I. with him - a chap called Backhouse. We've already had a preliminary discussion and agreed he's to concentrate on … well … I was going to say … the 'Irish Uncle' … but we might as well call him by his proper name now we know who he is. Anyway Le Saux and Backhouse will stick to him only for the moment, with you as 'observer' watching the interviews through a TV relay as they don't have 'one way glass' over at Steyning where the interview will be carried out.'

'Not here Sir?'

'What, with a non-stop procession of swivel-heads queuing up to watch? No Steyning'll be better, and it's nearer to Mrs Sommerton's should they need to go there. I also want you and your team to continue with the others lines of enquiry, stopping short if they appear to be bringing you anywhere near Doctor Moss. Let's hope we can get this all cleared up soon so you can get back to finding the man you're after.'

Reynard couldn't stop himself. 'Ha.'

It was enough; Bradshaw's annoyance showed immediately, and he sniffed in a great breath of air and glowered. 'You think that's funny?

'No Sir, I do not.' said Reynard, regretting the smile but not the sentiment which had prompted it. 'I'm sorry if it came out that way. It's just you said 'get back to finding the man I'm after' when, if Doctor Moss *is* guilty, I've already found him.'

'Don't be so pedantic, Foxy, you know what I mean. Now go and do something for ten minutes or find Le Saux and have a cup of tea with him. Whatever you do, be back here at two on the dot. Right?'

'Right, Sir.'

'And don't forget; as far as Doctor Moss is concerned Le Saux will be calling the shots. I want you to keep well out of it until we see what's what.'

'I won't interfere, Sir. And I'll take your advice and talk to my team now, either here or on the 'phone; we have to press on with the rest of our enquiries. Furness, the lad from Shoreham, has already found one of the cars we were looking for and everything's indicating the suspect who owned it, the alleged rapist you put us onto, Herbert McCloskey, has fled to France. I'll be in touch with the French Authorities later today.'

'OK, off you go then.'

***

The meeting with Le Saux and Backhouse took place in Superintendent Bradshaw's office, and lasted right through until five o'clock at which point a strategy had been agreed. It was much in line with the one the Super had outlined to Reynard earlier in the day. 'OK,' he said, 'so we're all set. You can make yourself scarce now D.C.I. Reynard. Avoid contact with anyone else in this station until we have Doctor Moss in custody … in fact go home. As to bringing the doctor in for questioning I think, D.S. Le Saux, you should make your move at the crack of dawn or earlier tomorrow. I've warned Steyning their cell will be required and hope they don't arrest anyone or take in a drunk during the night. Provided this all goes smoothly the initial interview ought to be taking place sometime tomorrow morning. Right?'

'Right Sir.' they all said.

Friday 19th February

The Interview Room, Steyning Police Station, Sussex. Friday. 19th February 2007. 11.15. a.m.

Doctor Moss, dishevelled and unshaven after a sleepless night at home and five hours in Steyning's only custody cell, was sitting at a table conversing quietly with his solicitor Mr Barry Townsend when Detective Chief Superintendent Charles Le Saux and D.I. 'Willie' Backhouse accompanied by a Police Constable in uniform came into the interview room. The minute they entered he fell silent and dropped his head to his chest. He looked sallow faced and bewildered.

D.C.S. Le Saux nodded across the table at the two seated men and took a chair facing them. Inspector Backhouse took the other one and leaning forward turned on the interview recording apparatus to introduce those present.

In the next room, all set to watch the proceedings on a TV Monitor sat D.C.I. Reynard, D.S. Groves, P.C. Best, and P.C. Furness, the four people who'd brought the investigation to this point but handed it over when conflicting loyalties loomed. Reynard, anxious to extract as much as possible from the interview Le Saux was conducting, and to keep his team in touch with what was going on, had decided to bring them all in to hear it.

Le Saux was the first to break the silence. 'For the benefit of the tape, please confirm you are Police Surgeon Doctor Gordon Emmerson Moss and you are a forensic pathologist attached to Sussex Constabulary.'

Moss raised his head momentarily and gave the superintendent a weak smile. 'I am.'

'D.I. Backhouse and I have now taken over the investigation into the death of Charlotte Sommerton at her home at Upper Beeding on the 13th of February 2010 and of her daughter, Rosaleen Sommerton, in or near Fyling Park sometime during the night of the14th/15th of February 2010. Do you understand?'

'I do; D.C.I. Reynard and I have been friends for years. I knew someone else would be brought in.'

Le Saux nodded. 'Right then, before we start looking for answers Doctor Moss, do you want to volunteer a statement or say anything regarding either of these deaths?'

Moss glanced at his solicitor, lifted his eyebrows, and got a slight nod in return. 'I was in the house when Mrs Sommerton died.' he said, 'I wasn't actually with her when she collapsed, not physically there you understand, not in the same room that is to say, though I was with her a few minutes after she'd died. I certainly didn't kill her.'

'And Rosaleen Sommerton?'

Moss looked across at his solicitor again. This time he was answered with a vigorous shake of the head prompting a reply of: 'No comment.'

Le Saux glared at him for a moment and said nothing. Then, clearing his throat, went on: 'In that case we'll take the death of Charlotte Sommerton first … carry on Inspector.'

Backhouse edged his chair forward, leaned cross armed on the table, and smiled. 'We need to be familiar with *all* the facts doctor, every single one, right from the start, even though you may have already been over the same ground in conversations you've had from time to time with D.C.I. Reynard. Do you understand? We've read the case notes but as you well know, having been involved in many investigations in the past yourself, it's not the same as getting the information first hand. So while it's a nuisance, we'll be going over it all again. We have to … for your sake as well as our own … right?'

The solicitor remained silent but Moss, responding to the friendly approach, was happy to answer. 'I haven't discussed my personal connection to the Sommerton family with anyone, and specifically not with D.C.I. Reynard … but yes … go on … I do understand; where do you want me to start?'

'We need to know everything … every little detail. So why don't you begin with how you came to know Mrs Charlotte Sommerton?'

Moss drew a deep breath. 'Well … I *didn't* really know her … I'd never met her, though …'

Le Saux raised his hand. 'Don't worry about Rosaleen for the moment. Stick to your relationship with Charlotte.'

Moss shrugged his shoulders. 'As I said… I didn't have one … a relationship, that is. I only heard of her for the first time a couple of months ago when I was in Ireland.'

'In Ireland … yes … why were you there … on holiday?'

'I'm Irish … I come from Ireland.'

'Really, you don't sound Irish to me … go on.'

'Well I am … I was born there on the farm *my* father inherited from *his* father. It's the way things are done in Ireland … father to son; father to son, and so on.'

'Nothing odd there; agricultural property here nearly always gets passed down through a son as well, doesn't it?'

'In Ireland the eldest son generally gets the place together with the responsibility of looking after his mother and any younger brothers and sisters who are still at home. But I'm not the eldest son. When my father died, my older brother Gerald got it.'

'I see, and you and the others got nothing.'

The doctor laughed. 'There are no others … just Gerry and me. My parents only ever had two children. I'd already left home and was half way through medical school when it was obvious he was going to get the place.'

'Were you envious?'

'Envious? No. There was no question of envy; I suppose I'd always known it would go to him, it's the custom. As it happens I didn't want it anyway; the money my parents had provided for my education was going to give me the career I wanted. It was more than enough compensation for not getting a farm I didn't want. To be frank I thought Gerry got the worst of the deal. He was stuck with a job he hated in a place he couldn't stick. He'd much rather have had the freedom I had. In fact long before then when he was twenty three, he went as far as leaving home, walked away from everything including his rights; said he hated the place.'

'Which left you sitting pretty?'

'It did not, I was about to start at medical school. The last thing I wanted was to be on the farm helping my father.'

'But if you had, you'd have got the place wouldn't you? After all your brother had gone; thrown his hat at it.'

'It's possible it would have come to me I suppose … but I didn't want it. I loathed the life my parents had, constantly struggling to make a decent living out of rotten boggy land, and I wasn't the slightest interested in farming. I wanted to be a doctor.'

'You parents must have been upset, disappointed even, your brother had gone and you weren't interested?'

'I dare say they were … but for their own reasons. We weren't a close knit family. We each lived in our own space. There was little enough of what you might call 'family life'.'

'So what happened? Did your …'

Le Saux tapped the desk. 'This isn't getting us anywhere. We're not interested in all this stuff about his family. Let's get back to Charlotte Sommerton.'

Backhouse, untroubled by the impatience his superior was showing, and determined to pursue the line he was following, compromised by suggesting the conversation might be about to bring them to Charlotte Sommerton.

'It is.' said Moss. 'My 'connection' to Charlotte Sommerton only existed because of my brother.'

'Alright.' said Le Saux, 'but speed it up a bit.'

Moss tried to force a smile but failed and started to speak again. 'As I was saying, my brother left home in seeming disregard for his rights of inheritance.'

'But that wasn't the way it worked out in the end?'

'No. He got as far as London and he soon had a job *and* a girl-friend. When he wrote home and told us I thought … we all thought … he'd kissed Ireland goodbye. I was just about to start at college as I told you, and I was worried to death about the way things seemed to be turning out, as were my parents. I can remember my mother begging me to go to London to find him and persuade him to return home.'

Le Saux shifted impatiently in his seat, 'Come on … come on … For Goodness's sake - Charlotte Sommerton.'

'I'm getting to her now.' said Moss 'You told me you wanted the whole story; I'm giving it to you.'

Le Saux nodded, but Backhouse knew he was about to explode and made another attempt to hurry the story along. 'OK doctor … so?'

'So, after three years my brother *did* return to Ireland and he *did* join my father on the farm. We could never fathom why he changed his mind and he wouldn't talk about it. In all honesty I don't think he understood why he'd left in the first place or come back in the second; he hated farming.'

'So in due course he inherited the place lock stock and barrel?'

'A long time afterwards; Dad lived until 1996.'

'So when he eventually got it he took on the responsibilities which went with it … your mother and so on?'

'Yes and No. He got the farm alright, but my mother had died some years earlier and, as he'd never married, he only had himself to think of.'

'And at this stage you were …?'

'Moving into forensic work and thinking of a career with the police. I'd been home the odd time of course, and every time I did I was thankful I wasn't the eldest; Gerry had a rotten life.'

'Couldn't make any money out of the poor land?'

'Not only that, no … he just didn't like the farming life … I actually thought he'd sell up.'

'Which would have left you …?'

'Exactly where I was. The farm was his to do what he liked with. I'd had my education.'

'And he'd no wife or family?'

'No, in fact he almost became a recluse … a crusty old bachelor. The local kids were all a bit scared of him, I believe.'

'So there was no woman in his life other than this girl in England and that was years before?'

'Not as far as I was aware there wasn't.'

'And then he died in a farmyard accident?'

'He did; and I went over to decide what to do with the property which, I assumed would come to me as there was no one else.'

'But you were wrong?'

'Was I ever?' 'It appeared he'd been married to his girlfriend in England all along.'

'And neither you or your parents knew.'

'It was a hell of a shock.'

'That you weren't going to get the farm or that he was married?'

'Both. Can we stop for a bit … I need a drink?'

'I think we all do, and I want to check something anyway,' said Le Saux, turning to the constable seated behind him and asking him to see if he would rustle up some tea. 'I'm going to have a word with Foxy, next door,' he whispered to Backhouse as he left the room, I'll be back in a minute.'

After Le Saux and the Constable had gone Backhouse sat back, folded his arms, closed his eyes, and tried to appear disinterested. Moss slipped into a motionless mode too, with his eyes wide open staring into the distance. On the other hand Townsend, his solicitor, was busy. He spent the whole time they waited for the tea to come, scribbling notes in the margins of his brief with a thin gold propelling pencil.

Reynard greeted Le Saux with a smile as soon as he stepped into observation annex. 'It's going well at the moment Sir, isn't it? But I can't help feeling sorry for poor old Mossy.'

'Mossy?'

'Gordon Moss … the doc. He's known as Mossy to his friends, poor devil.'

'Poor devil … now wait a bit. The information you've given us leaves it open that he might have killed at least one person … maybe two, am I right?'

Reynard shook his head. 'No Sir, we never got as far as formally investigating him; all this about him being her uncle only came out yesterday. Christ, I've known him for years … I can't believe he killed anyone, despite all these silly little coincidences which might indicate to some people that he did.'

'You're getting soft.'

'I'd rather be soft than wrong, Sir.'

'What about you three?' asked Le Saux, addressing Sergeant Groves and Constables Best and Furness. Come on speak up … anything come out so far which sounds different to what he's ever said previously in your presence?'

'No Sir,' they replied in unison.

'We'd better press on then.' said Le Saux, as he swung round to return to the interview. 'Let's see what he has to tell us about this relationship with Charlotte he says he didn't have. Keep your ears open you lot, he'll make a slip sooner or later.'

'You'll be lucky.' murmured Best, which brought a reproving look from Reynard.

Two minutes later, with everyone in their place again, the constable appeared in the interview room with a tray of mugs full of tea. 'Ready?' asked Backhouse, turning on the recorder as soon as the mugs had been passed round. 'Now

Doctor, back to Charlotte Sommerton … we got as far as you not knowing your brother was married to her and the shock it gave you … right? Tell us a bit more about that.'

'I got a call from the Irish Police, the Garda, from the town near where we lived - Templederry; it's in County Tipperary, on the south side of Lough Derg, which is part of the Shannon river system. They told me there'd been an accident at the farm and Gerry had been killed.'

'What sort of an accident?' asked Le Saux.

'A farmyard accident, sadly they're quite common. Apparently he'd been cutting up the branch of a tree which had fallen in a gale two winters ago. He'd hauled it up to the yard with the tractor and was cutting it up with an electric power saw. He must have slipped, cut the cable and electrocuted himself. I've heard of similar accidents before.'

'No chance of foul play being involved?'

'No Inspector, none whatsoever.'

'And he was on his own?'

'He was always on his own. To be truthful he went a bit strange with no company … talked to himself all the time.'

'So you went over to Ireland?'

'The next day.'

'And?'

'And I found everything as I expected until I started to go through his desk … that's when I discovered about his marriage. It gave me a hell of a shock because … not to put too fine a point on it … '

'You weren't going to get the farm.'

'Exactly and she wasn't even family, not real family … she'd never been to Ireland.'

'You assumed this of course.'

'I suppose I did but it's not all. On my way home I'd stopped at 'Monkey' Mooney's garage at Scarna to pick up milk and a few things I'd need when I got to the house. 'Monkey' was leaning on the counter reading an article in that week's issue of the Nenagh Guardian, our local paper. It was all about the new development plan for the area. He told me everyone was expecting increases in the value of land bordering the lake … huge increases … and we've got a quarter of a mile of water frontage! God Almighty … all those years the family's slogged away barely making ends meet and now after they've gone it might be worth a couple of million and someone else, a total stranger, was in line to get it.' I was livid I confess, absolutely bloody livid.'

'At who … your brother, his wife, yourself?'

Moss drew in a deep breath. 'I don't know … everyone I suppose … including myself. After all it would have been *mine* if I'd given up college and stayed at home at the time Gerry left and was living over here. He'd never have gone back if I'd been established there with Dad.'

Le Saux grinned. Assuming it was confirmed Charlotte Sommerton was the girl Gerry married years all those years before they had a clear motive for her death. Moss had killed her: his greed, his envy, and his jealousy, had brought about her death. She was going to get all the money which he thought rightfully his. It was as clear a reason for murder as they'd ever get. 'That's it then,' he said, thumping the table so hard with the flat of his hand he made the mugs bounce. 'You killed her to get her out of the way didn't you? And you killed Rosaleen for the same reason … she was your brother's daughter.'

Moss dropped his head wearily 'No, no, no you've got it all wrong … that's not it.'

'I think we have you.' said Le Saux, bouncing his papers together on the desk top, a pointer he often used to indicate the end of a session 'All this wealth going to Charlotte or to Rosaleen … and you couldn't swallow it so you killed them both.'

Moss lifted his head. 'No I didn't, it was far from certain either of them was entitled to it … I couldn't find his will for a start, nor could his solicitor.'

Le Saux almost laughed. 'So what! It won't matter in the long run. Even if he died intestate she or Rosaleen would still have got it. Didn't you ask his solicitor?'

'Of course I did … I just told you … he didn't have a will. He said he'd tried to get Gerry to make one but he'd refused. People do. There's no will; you can take it from me there's no will. But there were letters. I found a lot of letters … letters he'd received from Charlotte … over a long period of time … thirty years or more.'

'Which we can produce.' said Mr Townsend. 'They present a very odd slant on the relationship between Doctor Moss's brother Gerald and his 'so called' wife, Charlotte Sommerton.'

Backhouse shot back in his chair. 'What d'you mean 'so called'? Were they not married after all? Was Charlotte killed for nothing?'

'We have reason to believe we can prove Charlotte Sommerton was not, and never has been, Gerald Moss's wife … the relationship they 'manufactured' was false - a subterfuge to create a respectable back ground for their illegitimate daughter Rosaleen.'

'What?' said Backhouse, rising from his chair. 'They made it all up?'

Le Saux, equally surprised by what he was hearing raced through the notes he'd made when talking to Reynard the previous afternoon, but found no reference to the new turn of events. 'Wait a minute,' he said, holding up his hand, 'it looks to me as though we're into new territory here … there's been no mention of this before. What's clear is that you had some very solid reasons to wish Charlotte Sommerton and Rosaleen Sommerton dead and out of the way. I even wonder if you knew of them and their connection to your brother all along and decided to eliminate them before anyone else uncovered the secret.'

'I did no such thing. I knew Gerry had had a girl-friend in England years ago but I'd no idea who she was until I read the letters, and I'd never heard her name mentioned or seen it written down until I went over to clear things up after Gerry died.'

'What about Rosaleen Sommerton? You knew her, didn't you? You told D.C.I. Reynard.'

'I knew her slightly. Not in the context of being my niece I hasten to say but because my wife, who reads her column every week, was always talking about her and I'd also met her at a few charity functions my wife organised on which Rosaleen was reporting.'

Townsend, alarmed at what Moss might be about to say grabbed his arm. Moss hesitated then shook his head. 'Sorry, Chief Superintendent, as you can see I've been advised against saying anything regarding Rosaleen Sommerton.'

Le Saux was furious and banged his fist on the table. 'You killed her didn't you, you bastard … you killed her … Rosaleen Sommerton, your own niece, you strangled her in the car park at Fyling Castle and you dragged her body through the hedge and buried her in the snow.'

Moss didn't like it and reacted immediately. He straightened up out of the slumped position he'd been in for most of the interview and leapt to his feet. Townsend did the same; and alarmed at his client's behaviour and fearing he'd say something incriminating, he grabbed his arm for the second time and begged him to sit down. For a moment Moss looked as though he was going to refuse but then, as suddenly as he'd risen, he sat down again. 'No comment' he said.

Backhouse turned to Le Saux, who was still red in the face, and raised an eyebrow.

'Go on.' said Le Saux.

Backhouse leaned forward and stared into his empty tea cup but said nothing for a while; he, like Foxy Reynard, was 'a long pause' man. A full thirty seconds passed without anyone saying a word. Backhouse remained quite still, so did Le Saux as his complexion returned to normal. Townsend recognised the tactic and drew in a breath to speak, but Backhouse held up his hand and silenced him. Only Moss gave any really positive reaction: he started drumming the fingers of both of his hands on the table top.

Next door in the adjacent room, D.C. Best couldn't resist responding to the tension. 'He's reading the leaves … would you believe it … the inspector's reading the bloody tea leaves … look at him.'

'Shut up,' said Reynard.

Backhouse leaned towards Moss and slowly delivered his summation. 'So what you're saying is this, Doctor … you knew of Rosaleen Sommerton … but had nothing to do with her death … and while you didn't know her mother at all …you might have been present or nearby when she died. Am I right?'

'Right.' said Moss. 'That is correct. That is the situation.'

'OK. So back to Charlotte. You found these letters?'

'Yes. They were all clearly written by her to keep Gerry au fait with the progress of Rosaleen's life, right from when she was born up to the present. They looked to me more like a report from one interested party to another than a letter from a wife to her husband; there was no warmth in them at all. She addressed him 'Dear Gerald', and signed off 'Yours Sincerely, Charlotte Sommerton.' There was no sign of affection, no mention of love … just a string of facts about Rosaleen - it was more like a school report than a letter.'

'From which you deduced …?' asked Le Saux.

'From which I deduced they neither loved nor hated each other … they respected each other sufficiently to let Rosaleen come into the world, but not much more. I hadn't seen Gerry's letters to her at that stage of course, only Charlotte's to him, which I found in a kitchen drawer he'd seemed to have reserved for them … there was nothing else in the drawer with them.'

'Odd.'

'Very, but as I worked through the letters - which Mr Townsend has now, I eventually tumbled to what I believe to be the reason for the correspondence. I mean … if they'd loved each other they'd have lived together, wouldn't they? And if they'd no interest in each other they'd not have written the letters in the first place.'

'So why d'you think they kept up the correspondence … I presume he wrote to her frequently?'

'Less frequently than she wrote to him. I didn't know that until she showed me the file of letters the day I called to see her some weeks after Gerry died. Most of the letters were copies of hers to him. She told me she'd fabricated the marriage and the desertion for Rosaleen's sake, and he'd gone a long with it.'

'Backhouse shook his head. 'I don't get it; he walked out leaving her pregnant and yet she seems to have born him no resentment.'

'I don't think he knew she was pregnant when they parted. He must have got quite a shock when she wrote and told him she'd had a baby.'

'And she made no claim on him? That's hard to credit.'

'It's how it was, believe me. She bore him no resentment. From the way she told me the story I concluded that, daft as it was, she was somehow grateful to him, happy to be what we now call a 'Single Mum' instead of being locked into marriage neither wanted just to satisfy society's demands. I've even been drawn to think she set it all up.'

'What d'you mean, she lured him into her bed?'

'I think she did. From what she told me, and the way she talked about him, I got the distinct impression she'd selected him. Set out to find a man of a certain type to father the child she was desperate to have, one who would not expect or require to be otherwise included in her life or that of the child. She was looking for a stud … and Gerry came along - tall dark handsome and so on - and a charmer to boot. She was the escape he was looking for; he was sexual partner she needed.'

Le Saux scratched his head and shook it from side to side. 'It sounds so outlandish it's probably true. Charlotte

Sommerton was some schemer … and your brother was a lucky man. Amazing … if you're right.'

'I think I am; I've given it enough thought. It's not too difficult to understand, they adopted a plan to fit their circumstances to the social sensitivities prevalent at the time.'

'By which you mean?'

'She knew society wasn't ready to accept what we now call a 'Single Mum', but had no problem with a deserted wife who had a child. Once she had it square in her mind, she implied she wrote to Gerry and got his agreement. After that it only took a few harmless untruths to get a birth certificate showing 'Charlotte Sommerton' as the baby's mother and 'Gerald Sommerton' as her father.'

'So Charlotte used her maiden name as her married name and then told everyone her husband had deserted her … very clever.' said Le Saux. 'And no problems provided he agreed to the subterfuge.'

'Which he did. It was a better solution than abortion, which he might have insisted on, and everyone was happy.'

'You still haven't told us why you went to call on her.'

'I wanted to meet her. I was curious.'

'And it all came out.'

'Not straight off. Not the first time I went, that was only a brief call. It was on the second occasion a week later, the day she died - last Saturday - when as you say 'it all came out'.'

'By her I suppose you mean Charlotte, not Rosaleen?' asked Backhouse, who'd listened with increasing disbelief as the story of Rosaleen's beginnings unfolded.

'Yes, of course, Charlotte.'

'And how did she take it the first time you met her - the news Gerry had died - was she upset?'

'I wouldn't say she was distraught but she *was* upset. When she was more composed, we talked.'

'About?'

'I told her I wanted to meet Rosaleen.'

'I'll bet she didn't like that.'

'She didn't. She told me leave her alone, she'd tell her in due course.'

'Did you believe her?'

'Of course I didn't. I decided to bide my time and try again on another occasion. I thought she was being ridiculously defensive about the whole affair.'

'So you never called on Roz to introduce yourself?'

'Well I …'

Mr Townsend grabbed his arm and shook his head.

'Sorry. As you see I'm being advised not to answer you.'

'We'll leave that for the moment then and go back to Mrs Sommerton. Maybe she *wanted* the years of pretence to come to an end. Maybe she was *planning* to tell Roz about her father but simply hadn't worked out how to go about it.' Backhouse said, stifling a yawn.

'Yes, quite possibly, she was certainly much less belligerent regarding the disclosure of the information to Roz when I drove over to see her last Saturday evening than she had been the first time; she asked me if I'd like a cup of tea … I said I would. The kitchen was next to the room I was in and we carried on the conversation through the open doorway, and that's when it all came out - the whole story. Oddly she never asked me about Gerry's will though she must have wondered how Rosaleen stood with regard to his estate. And then, just as we were finishing our tea she started to tremble … an understandable reaction to tension she was feeling I thought.

She asked to be excused for a minute and went out into the kitchen. A minute or two later I heard a crash and rushed though. She was lying on the floor unconscious. I suspected she'd suffered a cardiac arrest. She was breathing unevenly and her pulse was weak and fluttering … typical symptoms of Arrhythmia. I wondered if she any history of heart trouble and looked in her hand bag for pills which might give me a clue. There were none. When I bent to check her again I realise how serious her condition was. When I came back from the car with my bag a minute or two later, she was dead. To die in this manner is not unusual; I've seen it many times before. And then I committed the only crime to which I'm prepared to admit. I left her where she was, went out to my car, and drove home.'

'And you made the call for an ambulance on the way, without disclosing your identity.'

'That's right.'

'And she died naturally; you didn't kill her?'

'My unexpected presence and the subject of our discussion may have been a contributory factor, but I didn't kill her. When I found myself back there a few hours later in my official capacity I had a chance to look around, and soon found her medication, confirming her heart irregularities.'

'Hmm.'

'You sound doubtful Inspector?' said Moss.

'Of course I'm doubtful.' Backhouse replied.

'Why?'

'I've just been reading the post mortem report.'

'And?'

'You bloody signed it.' he said. 'You carried out the post mortem medical examination yourself without disclosing to anyone you had a very relevant connection to the deceased, and had seen her the afternoon she died. Of course I'm suspicious. Wouldn't you be?'

'Oh Christ … I've been stupid, really stupid in hoping I could cover up my involvement. But I didn't kill her. Get someone else to check the body … you'll only wind up with a corroboration of what I've told you.'

'Really. It looks to me as though you killed her, and hid the fact with a falsified medical report knowing it was unlikely to be contradicted.'

Le Saux, well-known for his *im*patience, surprisingly intervened. 'Perhaps we should take another break, gentlemen.'

'I'd like to request we leave it over until tomorrow, Superintendent; my client is completely exhausted.' said Townsend, by then as pale as Moss was.

Le Saux glowered. 'Half an hour.' he said, 'No more. And then we'll move on to talk about Rosaleen.'

As soon as he got out of the room Le Saux went to seek out Reynard; there were urgent things to discuss before the interview got going again; but Reynard wasn't there.

'Looking for the Governor, Sir?' asked Best, trying to be helpful. 'He's gone down to the front office with Sergeant Groves to take a call from Bristol. The police down there have dug something up.'

'Dug something up? Any idea what?' asked Le Saux.

'Not a clue, Sir.' Best replied, a big beaming smile on his face. 'He shot off in a hell of a rush, with the Sergeant chasing after him. He said he hoped he hadn't got it all wrong … that's all I can tell you.'

With Reynard unavailable Le Saux went instead to the office down the corridor, which had been temporarily assigned to him. Backhouse, his notes open on his lap, was already there waiting. 'What do you make of it all then, is he guilty or stupid?'

'God knows! The whole story about Charlotte's death happening so conveniently for him is so damned improbable I'm inclined to think he made it up knowing it was unlikely to be challenged. On the other hand, he's an intelligent man and he must have known it would all catch him up sooner or later. No I feel I'm on the verge of agreeing with Foxy, who's shot off somewhere incidentally, though I wasn't earlier … this Moss chap doesn't actually give me the impression …'

'Of being Charlotte's killer … I agree. Nor can I see the likelihood of any forensic evidence being found which would support the idea she died of anything other than natural heart failure. She'd a long history of heart problems, we know it from her own G.P. who confirmed she could have collapsed and died at any time if put under stress. No … I think our suspect's in the clear regarding being responsible for her actual death … unless he let her die … but I don't know how we'll prove it. Leaving her unattended with the slightest possibility she was still alive is going to bring his house down though. It'll cost him his job surely, and maybe his career. I'm going to have a word with the D.P.P to see if he can be charged with anything; we can't see him go 'scot free''

'He's finished as a doctor for sure.'

'Oh yes. So, what'll we do now … move on to Rosaleen? We've a better chance of collaring him for her death; after all he had a good reason to want *her* dead because her inheritance rights were senior to his.'

Backhouse agreed. 'Charlotte wasn't his rival for the farm because she wasn't either the married or the common law wife of his brother Gerald. Rosaleen, on the other hand, was his brother's daughter, even though she didn't know it, and was clearly entitled to first claim on his estate. We're not going to get much help from Moss though are we? Not like we did when he was talking about Charlotte. He's told us repeatedly he won't cooperate with us over Rosaleen.'

'Which in itself raises suspicions.' said Le Saux, standing as if to go.

Backhouse shoved his notes in his briefcase and stood as well. 'Start again?'

'Two minutes. I must see what Foxy's up to first and then we'll get on with it.'

Backhouse nodded and made for the interview room while Le Saux made another attempt to speak to Reynard. However as soon as he entered the room in which the inspector had been he realised he was still missing.

'Want me to fetch him, Sir?' asked Best.

'No, it'll wait.' Le Saux replied, and went back to his place in the interview room, speaking as he entered. 'Right … before we get into Rosaleen Sommerton's death, I'd like to clear up one last thing regarding Charlotte's. You mentioned letters several times earlier, Doctor Moss; and you Mr Townsend, told us you had a number of them which support the evidence Doctor Moss gave us - particularly in regard to the relationship between Charlotte Sommerton and his brother; am I right?'

'You are. We have the letters Charlotte wrote to Doctor Moss's brother Gerald.' said Townsend, 'I got the solicitor in Templederry to collect them from the farm and send them over to me by courier. They arrived yesterday afternoon.'

'And the corresponding ones you saw in Charlotte Sommerton's house doctor, where are they?'

Moss looked at him blankly. 'I'm not sure. I saw them the first time I called but not the second, maybe she'd given them to Roz.'

'You mean she'd changed her mind about maintaining the secrecy surrounding Rosaleen's father after your first visit?

'It appeared so. She said Rosaleen had called up to see her on Thursday as usual and she'd told her everything, braced herself and given her the whole story.'

'And how had Rosaleen taken it?'

'Indifferently, 'quite uninterested as to who her father was,' Charlotte said.'

'Strange.'

'That's what I thought. Anyway, I seem to remember she said she'd given Rosaleen the file to take away. It's probably at her flat, or in her office.'

'The complete correspondence?'

'Yes, her letters had all been typed and she'd a carbon copy of each which she'd filed with the answers she'd got from him. I saw them all.'

'You say 'file' … what sort of file?'

'A grey one … with a red spine. The sort you use in an office … 'lever arch' I think they're called.'

'There is no mention of a lever arch file being found at Rosaleen Sommerton's, but I'll get a man round to see if he can find it. So Rosaleen was up at her mother's after you'd called the first time?'

'Yes.'

'Why did you go back to see Charlotte?'

'I was going to ask her to change her mind. You know - agree I could introduce myself to Rosaleen - but she said 'not yet.'

Townsend who'd been carefully following the exchanges and who was getting progressively more and more apprehensive regarding his client's opening up so much in response to the questions, reached forward and tapped Moss's arm again. He reacted instantly. 'Yes … sorry Mr Townsend. 'Er, Superintendent, I can't say any more.'

Backhouse ignored him, and continued to press. 'Come on doctor, this is in your interest if you've been giving us the truth. Are you sure Rosaleen had the file; these letters are as important to you as they are to us and so far we only have your word they exist at all?'

'No comment.'

Le Saux leaned forward, glaring, 'Are you trying to tell us you didn't mind if Rosaleen found out about the farm when all the time you knew she'd greater rights to it than you? Come on Doctor Moss surely you don't expect us to believe that?'

'No comment.'

'No comment.' parodied Le Saux. 'No bloody comment!'

Backhouse blew his nose into a large red spotted handkerchief and returned it to his top pocket. 'Right, so let's talk about Rosaleen. Let's see what progress we can make with her murder for, whatever you may claim about the natural death of her mother, Rosaleen was killed unlawfully.'

Townsend opened his brief case and took out a single sheet of paper. 'At the beginning of this interview gentleman you invited my client to make a statement. He prepared this one in my presence yesterday. Nothing which has been said so far this morning in any way conflicts with this document which relates, in its entirety, to the death of Rosaleen Sommerton.'

'Taken your time producing it haven't you?' said Le Saux, making little attempt to hide his displeasure.

'My client's innocence with regard to Charlotte's death,' the lawyer went on, unperturbed by Le Saux's taunt, 'will be confirmed by any court assuming the D.P.P finds there is sufficient evidence to prosecute in the first place … which I doubt. Doctor Moss's innocence in the case of Rosaleen Sommerton's death however, is likely to be more difficult for us to prove … as will your ability to secure a verdict of guilty. In either event, complications arising from extraneous evidence will have to be sifted out. We are making a start on that process by offering you this statement written by Doctor Moss. In it you will find he admits he intended to visit Rosaleen again at some time in the future in the hope of being able to introduce himself as her uncle, he never expected to see her lying on the ground in Fyling Park with a policeman brushing snow off her face; it was a terrible shock to him.'

'How did he know the body on the ground was Rosaleen Sommerton, no one else did at that stage?'

'I believe he told you that already; he'd met Rosaleen at several local charity functions, organised by his wife, on which she was reporting.'

'Hmm.' murmured Le Saux, purposely sounding unconvinced.

'Well, as you can appreciate gentlemen, as soon as he saw her lying on the snow in the S.O.C.O. tent in Fyling Park he realised he was in a tricky situation and now, in retrospect, he wishes he'd told D.C.I. Reynard of his connection to the deceased there and then. However, in a badly judged moment of panic he didn't and things went from bad to worse. Before he had time to think of a way out of the muddle he'd created, he was trapped in it. He knew his silence would damn him eventually but he didn't know what to do. In the end he carried on with his job and hoped for the best, prayed his connection to Rosaleen would never be uncovered. Again, as you will find in the statement, he much regrets the embarrassing position in which he has put so many of his friends and colleagues.

When he last saw Rosaleen Sommerton alive it was just before Christmas, at a fundraiser in aid of the District Nurse, organised by his wife.

He did not kill her, and he knows of no reason why her life should have been brought to such a ghastly and untimely end.

In this statement, which I have just summarised, you will find my client's testimony in his own words.

One final thing as regards the farm. It's likely my client will inherit it in due course but the granting of probate, especially as intestacy is involved, is likely to be delayed for many months.'

When Townsend had finished he slowly looked around the table at each of the others in turn. Doctor Moss, had his head bowed and his eyes closed, unable to face anyone. Le Saux was glaring at him, so was Backhouse.

The Black Bull Hotel, Steyning.
Friday 19th February 2010. 1.55.p.m.

Reynard had taken the telephone call just as the interview ended. It was a long and surprising one and gave promise of a major advance in their investigations. After a few words of explanation to Le Saux who he saw coming out of the interview room with Backhouse, he collected his team together and they drove out to The Black Bull on the Brighton Road to have a discussion and make plans over a sandwich. Afterwards, and arising from the telephone call he'd just taken, Reynard accompanied by Groves intended to leave for Bristol, where they'd been invited to observe an interview scheduled for five o'clock. A man who might be the Irish driver Mrs McWilliam had seen driving off with Roz Sommerton had been arrested and was being held for questioning by the Avon and Somerset Police.

'While we're in Bristol,' he said to Best and Furness, 'you two can drive to the Globe office on Old Worthing Road and look through the lever back files you'll see lined up on the shelf in Roz Sommerton's office. Check every single one understand, from back to front; you know what you're looking for - a load of letters.

Serious Crimes Office,
Avon & Somerset Police,
Kenneth Steele House, Bristol BS2 2AS.
Friday 19th February, 2010, 4.56 p.m.

They'd travelled cross country instead of yielding to the temptation of using the motorways and were sitting in the waiting room with a waxed paper cup containing coffee they'd got from the machine at the door, waiting for Sergeant Brothers to collect them. It was he who'd telephoned Reynard and given him the information which had sent their pulses racing.

'Not bad for timing.' said Reynard, looking at his watch.

Groves swirled the drink round in her cup and peered at it with disgust. 'Ugh. I don't think much of this, Guv? And they've no decent biscuits to take the taste away either, we should have brought our own.'

'Shh.' said Reynard, looking through the open door and seeing a young and exceedingly tall man loping towards them. 'This'll be him,' he whispered, 'and by Golly he's a big 'un.'

Groves looked up as a six foot six bean pole of a man with the appearance of a teenager came bounding in. He was wearing a black leather bomber jacket over a white tee shirt and jeans and he had a huge and enthusiastic smile on his face. His whole appearance from the tufty light brown hair, which was sticking out at all angles as if it were trying to escape from his head, to the dirty untied runners on his feet, was more like that of an overgrown school boy than a police officer. 'D.C.I. Reynard … great.' he said, thrusting out his hand.

Reynard, taken aback by the overwhelming welcome, didn't respond.

'You are D.C.I. Reynard, I presume?' said the young man, fearing he'd made a mistake.

'Well I'm not Doctor Livingstone.' answered Reynard, taking the young man's hand and smiling mischievously. 'You'll be Sergeant Brothers …. *I presume*? This is Sergeant Groves.'

Brothers grinned. 'Make it Les.'

'Ah … right.' replied Reynard, allowing his smile to fade and making no effort to offer his own first name, or his nickname.

Brothers cottoned on immediately; "old school', gotcha!' he said to himself, turning to Groves and shaking her hand.

'And who's this 'bird' you've got in the cage for us?' asked Reynard. 'If he's who I think he is we'd very much like to have a chat with him.'

'I'll tell you about him in a minute, but I must have a cup of coffee first I've been here all night. And I'm not going to drink that machine muck.' he said, giving a meaningful glance at the drink Groves was holding in her hand. 'It's piss.'

Reynard smiled. 'I'll not argue with that and nor I am sure, will Sergeant Groves. Do you have a better alternative?'

Brothers didn't answer; he turned and waved them through the doorway. 'Up the stairs, first on the right, help yourselves; I'll be up in a minute.'

'He don't waste his words' said Reynard, as he and Groves mounted the stairs and went into the office Brothers had indicated. On top of the filing cabinet a Cona coffee jug, cosily nestled in its mantle, was delivering a wonderful and familiar aroma. Reynard's face lit up immediately. 'Not a bad chap this Sergeant Brothers - knew it the minute I saw him; and do I detect the aroma of Costa Rica - I do if I'm not mistaken. I bet he'll have something interesting to go with it too.'

'Biscuit man are you?' replied Brothers, who had come in quietly behind them. 'What d'you like Custard Creams? Garibaldis? Ginger Snaps? No, no, no of course not … I can see from your face … you're a bit of a specialist … a Hobnob man I dare say.'

Groves was in stitches by then and shook her head in mock reproof but Reynard, having rapidly re-assessed young Sergeant Brothers, was beaming. 'Right.' he said, once they'd settled; a mug of coffee in one hand and a chocolate Hobnob biscuit in the other. 'So tell us about this fella you've got.'

Brothers pulled a file from his desk and opened it. 'His name's John Edward Fogarty and he's been in our sights for months. He lives part of the time in …'

'Irish is he? Sounds like it with a name like Fogarty.'

'Irish, yes but he spends little time there other than on his boat, which is moored in a place called Kinsale. Most of the time when he's not travelling the world, he lives in a rented house in a village called Upton Cheney; it's half way between here and Bath. But we're fairly certain he also rents another place in The Marina Village in Brighton.'

'Does he indeed? He's never come up on our radar, what have you pulled him in for? You said something about illegal imports … facsimile goods from Asia, cheap copies of things made by well-known companies like Nike ... correct?'

'More or less. We've pulled him in for smuggling.'

Reynard burst into laughter. 'Smuggling? What 'brandy for the parson, baccy for the clerk' that sort of smuggling?'

'Ah dear old Rudyard Kipling … I learned him at school as well. No it's more serious … he's bringing in pharmaceuticals at the moment, but he's also into in clothes and perfume and anything else which he can get copied on the cheap. He trades in bogus goods and unauthorised clones of well-known brands. He gets them manufactured in India, or Thailand, or Indonesia, and the ships them here to be packaged before being sold on to gullible punters through a whole string of unscrupulous shopkeepers, street traders, and cut price drug stores.'

'So it's Glaxo, Gucci and Givenchy on the cheap?'

'Absolutely. Currently he's doing non- prescription weight loss tablets, you know - calorie burners, appetite suppressants, absorption blockers … that sort of thing. The stuff's all tarted up in magnificent packaging and at first sight, appears to have been made under licence from one of the big international pharmaceutical companies like Schering, or Pfizer, or Beecham. He gets the names of the licensing companies marginally adjusted in the small print so our job is just a bit more difficult. The average punter never sees the difference.'

'How come?' asked Groves, who was taking down notes. 'Give us an example?'

'Easy … Pffizer for Pfizer; Beacham for Beecham; and a beauty I saw the other day on some slimming pills - Merk, Sharp and Dohm for Merck, Sharpe and Dohme.'

'Hang on,' said Reynard. 'You haven't explained how you knew we were interested in Fogarty.'

'OK, here's what happened. My oppo who's attached to the nick at Crawley saw one of your lot had sent a circular round the division seeking information from anyone who'd come across a man you wanted to interview. The circular said he might be Irish, called 'Geoff', and he could be driving a big dark coloured 4x4 bearing a IRL sticker and a personalised English plate ending in 1697 or 1967. The memo had been on my colleague's desk for over a day when it dawned on him the guy who was wanted mightn't be called Geoff at all but 'JEF' - the nickname of the Irish fella *we're* watching, whose full name is John Edward Fogarty, and who drives an almost new Dark Blue Beamer 5X, with the registration number J E F 1697. Before he had time to contact you though, he heard we'd picked him up, so *he* rang me … and *I* rang you.'

'Right, got it;' said Groves, 'so back to Fogarty, how does he fit into the counterfeiting game you're investigating, I'd appreciate it if you …'

Brothers nodded. 'Join the dots? Sure. We reckon he's the 'smoother', the 'enabler'. He's high in the organisation, may even *be* the organisation as far as the U.K. is concerned. He's the one who keeps all the different elements of the operation running cohesively and unobtrusively. He's around when the goods come in and stays with them until they're delivered to one of his 'wholesalers'. H.M. Customs are the main body involved in the investigation but the Fraud Squad are in it as well … and various other interested technical bods. We in Bristol are involved as back up to the specialists, providing discrete surveillance whenever he's known, or thought to be, on our patch. There's another team, at Crawley which does the same thing when Fogarty's in their neck of the woods bringing in stuff through Gatwick or the Channel ports.'

'And staying in the Marina Village in Brighton - amazing;' said Reynard with a sniff, 'all this going on right under our noses and I've never heard anything about it.'

'Just as well ... our lads are meant to be under cover.'

'What d'you say his full name is again?' asked Groves

'John Edward Fogarty. He's in his late twenties or early thirties; a big heavy guy - built like tank. He drives this magnificent 4x4 BMW which he keeps in showroom condition, and he's a sharp dresser: fancy suits, silk shirts and ties, hand-made shoes ... the lot. Oh yes, John Fogarty's a 'smart cookie', as the Yanks would say. We've never been able to pin as much as parking ticket on him yet we know he's responsible for millions of pounds worth of crime and a hell of a lot of misery.'

'So how did you catch him in the end?'

'Noise.'

Reynard bent forward with laughter. 'God Almighty, 'noisy smuggler detained by Avon and Somerset Constabulary'. It'll look great on the stats won't it? We could do with something like that, something nice and juicy.'

'Yeah, yeah, yeah.' said Brothers, 'but we're grasping at anything, anything to get this bloody man out of circulation. With him out of the way the whole organisation will collapse ... crumble away. He *is* the organisation ... whether he owns it or not.'

'OK ... joking apart ... what happened to give you the opportunity to nab him, and how are you managing to hold him; he sounds like the sort who'd have a sharpish brief on the job?'

'He has, and you might soon find yourself having deal with her. Her name's Jasmine Joyce.'

'Oh ... her. Well, I suppose I should have guessed, she's always the one who pops up where the dodgy Irish, and Civil Rights nutters are in trouble. Yes, I know her alright; anyone with a television does: small bright and bloody clever with an

Indian immigrant mother and Irish republican father. She's damned clever and pretty successful … just my luck to find she's involved.'

'There you are then Chief Inspector, she's downstairs with Fogarty right now waiting for me to go down to them.'

'Briefly then ….'

'Very briefly: last night, coming up to midnight, one of our guys was sitting in a parked car down the road from Fogarty's house, keeping an eye on things and making sure if Fogarty went out we'd know where he was going and …'

'See who he was going to meet.' Groves added.

'Exactly. But he didn't go out … a load of people came instead, thirty or forty of them, and it was soon obvious he was having a party. As it progressed it must have been getting noisier, though our man couldn't hear anything he was too far away. Fogarty's neighbours, who'd suffered from his wild festivities before clearly could, and they rang Trinity Road nick and asked for a car to be sent round to quieten the festivities down. My man saw it arrive and naturally wondered what the hell was going on. When the driver got out of the squad car and went up to Fogarty's front door, my man got out of his car too and slowly stole up to see what was happening. Just as he got into a position where he had a good view, he saw Fogarty shove the copper back and slam the door in his face …. And then ... and then …' he said, struggling to find words which would accurately describe the next few dramatic moments as seen by his man who was hidden by a well-trimmed beech hedge. And then …'

Reynard wriggled on his seat. 'Ah come on Sergeant … don't keep us in suspense. It's not bloody play acting.'

'I know, I'm sorry; but I want to get this right.

Reynard nodded. 'Go on then.'

'The copper knocked on the door over and again until Fogarty re-appeared. When he did he lashed out. Hit the copper from the squad car full in the face and flattened him. Then turned round and went straight back in, slamming the door behind him.'

'He must have been high … it was stupid … he'd have known it was too, if he'd been in his right senses.'

'Oh I'm sure you're right there Sir; he'll be kicking himself now. But there it is … he played right into our hands with something which has nothing whatsoever to do with the business we're interested in. Anyway it seems the young copper had phoned in for help before he knocked the second time and luckily there was another car in the vicinity. It had been chasing a group of kids who were joy-riding and lost them. They sped round to Fogarty's and arrived just in time to see him punch our copper who'd knocked on the door.'

'Ha … great, so they took him in for assaulting a police officer?'

'They did and he's been our guest ever since … for the best part of … let me see …' Brothers looked at his watch 'best part of seventeen hours.'

'During which time your pal in Crawley spotted the connection with our investigation and rang you. Great - are you handing Fogarty over to me now?'

'No Chief Inspector,' said Brothers, 'not yet, we doing a bit of investigation of our own. Once Fogarty had been taken off and the guests had been sent home we had to secure the premises. After all we couldn't go off irresponsibly leaving the place open to burglary, could we?'

'You crafty buggers; you searched the house You took the opportunity he'd gifted you and turned the place over; went though it with a bloody magnifying glass I expect … you …'

'Well … yes … and we found a lovely big box of DVD's - mostly pornographic - but there were also some current movie hits and all the Harry Potters. There was a letter in with them which has disappeared *unfortunately!*. It was from the man in Hong Kong who'd sent them to Fogarty, indicating they were samples and asking if he'd be interested in bulk purchase. It's a good job the letter's somehow gone astray it might have helped him wriggle out of the charges we're hoping will put him in jail. Bit of luck for us … if you know what I mean.'

'Ah, what a shame!' said Reynard with a grin. 'And did you find anything which might help us?'

'I went back this morning and had another look ... and yes I have got a couple of things. We'll have to be careful how we use them though. Don't want to lose sight of our objective regarding the copycat goods or let him see our hand.'

'Flooding the market with counterfeit goods which infringe a few Health and Safety regulations or Patents Office rules, come on Sergeant, what planet are you on? We want him for murder. If you get a conviction he'll be out in five, maybe three provided Ms Wotsit does her stuff, and she will.. Help us to put him behind bars for murder and he'll be there for twenty years, we'll have done your job for you.'

Brothers was nodding even as Reynard spoke. 'Sadly, I'd worked that out for myself, Chief Inspector … which is why I rang you so quickly and asked you down. Now … here's what I suggest. I'll take a D.C. in with me, if I can find a spare one …'

'No, sorry for butting in … *here's* what we're going to do. You interview him about the noise, the assault, and the box of

DVD's you stumbled on when checking the house before locking it up. Show a strong interest in the 'porn' rather than the copied discs. You'll have to say something about them, of course, can't pretend you didn't see them at all, but let him think your main interest is the blue movies. Well stay out of it … just watch if you have the facility.'

Brothers nodded. 'See through wall, yes we do.'

'Good. I'll prime you with a few questions I need answered before I decide whether I'm ready for him. If things go the right way I'll get a message to you and you can release him … pending etcetera.'

'And you'll re-arrest him as he exits the station?'

'I will, Sir, with the help of God, and twenty little cockney firemen.'

'What?' asked Brothers, but before he got a reply he saw the twinkle in Groves' eye. 'Right,' he said, 'let's do it … let's nail this bastard.'

Interview room 'A' , Serious Crimes Office, Kenneth Steele House, Bristol BS2 2AS. Friday 19th February, 2010, 18.35 pm.

Present: Sergeant Leslie Brothers
Detective Constable Derek Brown
Mr John Edward Fogarty
Ms Jasmine Joyce.

John Fogarty and his solicitor Jasmine Joyce were seated and conversing when the other two came into the office. Brown sat down opposite Fogarty and having turned on the record machine, read out the names of those present from a slip of paper Sergeant Brothers had given him. When he'd done that he sat back and listened.

Brothers, a series of questions lined up in his mind, was about to start asking them when Jasmine Joyce, a five foot nothing feisty young woman of about thirty, with a sallow complexion and tulip cut jet black hair, carefully picked a hair from the sleeve of her black business suit and went straight into the attack. 'Sergeant, I don't know what we're doing here. My client has already apologised to the constable he rather stupidly struck and we have offered compensation. The matter is closed as far as we are concerned. Charge my client or release him; he's been in custody for over seventeen hours and he's been punished more than enough.'

'There are one or two things to be cleared up first Miss Joyce.' Brothers replied.

'What things? You've had all day to pose questions and here we are still waiting for you to decide if you are going to make a charge. What's the problem?'

'The problem is the box.'

Joyce turned to Fogarty and shrugged her shoulders as much as to say 'do you know what he's talking about?' but Fogarty just shook his head. 'You'll have to be more explicit.' she said to Brothers.

'The one we found on the dining room table full of DVD's, a very large number of which were pornographic and several others, including some Harry Potters, were counterfeit. What were you doing with them Mr Fogarty?'

Fogarty looked perplexed. 'Doing with them … nothing … some guy left them at my house last week on a day I wasn't there. My cleaning lady took them in. I knew nothing about them until I came home the next day. I'm not interested in that sort of stuff.'

'So why d'you think he left them with you?'

'Obvious isn't it … he wanted me to buy them … it's what the letter said anyway.'

'What letter, we found no …'

Miss Joyce, who'd been listening to them in silence, and with increasing disbelief, suddenly found her voice. 'Wait a minute Sergeant … am I to understand you went in and searched my client's home without his permission?'

'We went in to make sure everything was safe before we left, and to lock up. After all as we had Mr Fogarty in custody it would have been quite wrong for us to leave his home open to robbery. The officer who was checking the French windows in the dining room saw the open box on the table and noticed what was inside it. Now Mr Fogarty, you'll have to think of a better excuse for having this disgusting material than you've given us so far. Do you import them, distribute them, you must have fairly successful business, and these DVDs must be very profitable?'

Fogarty, trying to appear unconcerned by the grilling he was getting held out his hands, fingers splayed out, and examined his nails; then he folded his fingertips down to touch his palms, turned his hand over and examined them again. 'They're nothing to do with me.' he said.

'So what sort of business are you in … it must be a good one you appear to have plenty of money, a lovely five bedroom house with a big well-tended garden; a smashing 'Beamer' - a 5X no less and, as to clothes, well, we couldn't believe it when our chap came back and told us. Rows of Geive and Hawkes suits; drawers full of Turnbull and Asser silk shirts, ties by Cerruti …

'Don't forget my shoes; they're made by John Lobb in case he didn't notice. But so what? Everything's paid for, you can check.'

'Of course … we don't doubt it … nothing from Marks and Spencer's or Cotton Traders in your wardrobe. And everything paid for naturally ... the question is … where does all the money come from?'

'My client has independent means.' said Ms Joyce, but it was clear she was surprised by what she was hearing and unsure where the police questioning was leading. 'I can't see what this has to do with what happened last night.'

Brothers however, who was practically beaming by then, wasn't to be put off. 'So what are these independent means you have; where does your money come from ... you're not on social welfare obviously.'

Fogarty missed the dig at his pomposity, and shook his head. 'That's for poor people.'

'Which of course you are not. So where ….?'

'My folks … in Ireland; we had hotels … seven of them and two in France.'

'Oh yes, of course, you spend quite a bit of time in France don't you?'

'On and off.'

'And you go to Dubai as well pretty frequently.'

'I do go to Dubai yes … so what? Lots of people do.'

'Do you go alone? Are these holidays or what?'

'Holidays of course; I've no time for business.'

'Ah yes, our man saw photographs of you in some of the exotic places you visit.'

'Where is this going Sergeant?' asked Ms Joyce wearily. 'None of it is remotely connected to the incident regarding which you may, or may not, be about to raise a charge against my client. If you are … get on with it; if not you must let him go immediately.'

'Yes,' said Brothers, completely ignoring her. 'all sorts of places I'd like to go if I could afford it. And all sort of lovely girls went with you too, didn't they? Avril, Janice, Rosaleen, Portia, you pencilled their names on the back. You're a lucky chap Mr Fogarty; loads of money, loads of girls, and no need to work for any of it … I wish I were you.'

Ms. Joyce finally exploded 'Sergeant! For God's sake get on with it … charge him or release him.'

Brothers wrinkled up a smile. 'You can go Mr Fogarty; don't go punching any more policemen. You'll not get away with it next time. And, by the way, you'd better take the IRL sign off your BMW, it's English registered.'

'I'm not though.' said Fogarty. 'I'm Irish.'

'Fair enough.' replied Brothers, standing up and making for the door 'You'd better wear it then.'

As they left the room, and started to walk down the corridor leading to the main entrance, Brothers saw Reynard and Groves slip out of an office a bit farther down and walk ahead of them into the street.

***

Outside, hunched up against the cold and standing in slush, Reynard heard his phone ringing in his pocket. 'Damn,' he said, taking off his gloves and fishing the instrument out. 'It's Best.' he said to Groves after glancing at the screen. 'Good … good. Put it on my desk and we'll see you tomorrow. What … Jack Crowther … oh forget him, I know what he wants … no, on second thought, tell him he'll have his money in the morning, I'll be in early. I want you all in early … my office eight o'clock, right?'

'Here he comes.' said Groves.

As Fogarty and his solicitor came out through the door Reynard and Groves moved into their path.

'John Edward Fogarty?'

'Oh no … now what?' said Ms Joyce.

Reynard and Groves flashed their warrant cards. 'Are you John Edward Fogarty of Marina Village, Brighton?'

'I …'

'Do you know a woman called …'

Jasmine Joyce, hopping from one foot to the other in fury could stand it no longer. 'I don't know what you're up to officer, but my client has just been discharged and he lives in Upton Cheney, not Brighton. I must insist you stop harassing him … come on Mr Fogarty let's go.'

'Not so quick if you please Ms Joyce. I think you may have your facts mixed up. You do own, or have use of, an apartment you regularly use in Brighton Village don't you, Mr Fogarty?'

'It's not my home though.'

Ms Joyce slightly unsure of herself, made one more attempt to stop the questioning. 'He's told you … he lives in Upton Cheney. Look … Inspector is it?'

Reynard nodded. 'Detective Chief Inspector Reynard … and this is Sergeant Groves.'

'Right Chief Inspector,' said Ms Joyce.' There's obviously some mix up here and we can't stand out here in the street debating it. Can we talk inside?'

'Certainly we can.' said Reynard, 'Go ahead and see if we can use an interview room Sergeant, we'll be right behind you.'

Groves walked on as requested, followed by the diminutive solicitor with her burly client, who'd adopted an idiotic grin of self-satisfaction, following on behind her. Reynard brought up the rear.

By the time they'd all passed though the double swing doors Groves was at the desk talking to the desk Sergeant. At that very moment two police constables emerged from the corridor which served the custody suite. One of them stopped in his tracks when he saw Fogarty. 'Ha, in a spot of bother again are you Mr Fogarty?'

Fogarty's grin disappeared.

The P.C turned to his companion 'This is the hero who hit me last night.' he said, 'He thinks he's a big man with his big cars, his big house, and his big mouth. But he's all belt and no braces. He talks big and acts small. I'll have him soon and it'll make my day.'

Fogarty took a threatening step forward; Jasmine Joyce took one back, as did Groves. But Reynard, who could see what was coming a mile off put down his briefcase and stood still with his arms folded. He didn't have long to wait. Fogarty suddenly lunged forward and threw a mighty punch, flooring the policemen he'd hit the previous night again, and prompting the desk sergeant and the second constable to rush forward and grab him.

'And you think you've got problems!' said Ms Joyce to Reynard, as she looked despairingly at her client, by then bent over double with one of his arms forced up his back. 'I guess we'll be meeting again.'

'I rather think we will.' replied Reynard. 'And I look forward to it.'

Saturday 20th February

Sussex Police Major Incident Suite, Sussex House, Brighton Sussex. Saturday 20th February, 2010, 8.15. a.m.

They were all there; the Cona Coffee jug was bubbling gently, Groves was opening the Hobnob biscuits, and Reynard, watched by Best and Furness, was leafing through the lever arch file they'd brought from Roz's office … when Sergeant Crowther burst in.

'Where the hell have you been Foxy, you have me demented trying to get through to you. You never return my calls; you've ignored my text messages. For Christ's sake, I'm trying to help you mate.'

As he ranted on in frustration Reynard, took his wallet from his pocket and plucked out a ten pound note.

Crowther shook his head. 'I don't want your bloody money … I've found your victim's fiancé.'

Reynard slowly replaced the bank note in his wallet and looked up at Crowther. So did the others. 'Say that again,' he said, 'you've found her fiancé. What on earth are you talking about.'

'Make room.' said Crowther, 'I'll get a chair.'

Two minutes later, coffee and biscuits forgotten, Sergeant Crowther began: 'I've told no-one this, I wanted to give it to you first. But if you hadn't come in this morning I'd have had no choice but to give it to the Super. One way or another this news is now a day old and I couldn't have waited for you any longer.'

'OK, go on.' replied Reynard, leaning forward with his arms folded on his desk in front of him.

'Well you know I told you I'd lost my body?'

Reynard smiled but the others looked puzzled. 'Ah, it's just something between Sergeant Crowther and me,' he told them, 'a joke - forget it.'

'Yes, well it turned up the day before yesterday on the beach near Rottingdean.' said Crowther.

'Hang on while I explain,' said Reynard, going on to tell the others about the 'Miss Per' Crowther was looking for.

'Yes … well,' said Crowther, 'it wasn't a high priority, and as I'm run off me flamin' feet with the work I took of you, on top of my own, I didn't do much until the body turned up. All I'd done at that stage was collect a few facts from the parents of this man who'd been reported missing on Tuesday.'

'And he's the guy you think might be Roz Sommerton's fiancé. Who is he for a start?'

'His name's … can I have a coffee?'

'Pour him one.' said Reynard, 'In fact let's all have one … and a biscuit … this might take a while.'

As Groves reached across and poured the coffee, Crowther continued with his story. 'His name's Tony Simmonds.' he said, 'he lives … lived, sorry … in a flat over a shop he used as an office on the Marine Road half a mile beyond Trafalgar Terrace. He's been in an 'on and off' relationship with Roz Sommerton for three years according to his Dad.'

'He must be the builder Marion mentioned.' said Groves. Big chap is he?'

'Yes but …'

'And good looking?'

'I suppose so, it all depends.'

'Let Sergeant Crowther get on with it Sergeant.' said Reynard. 'Carry on … how did you find out he was associating with our victim?'

'For a start he's an architect not a builder and he has a young student, a work experience undergraduate from the university, who helps him on Thursday and Friday afternoons in exchange for extra tutoring. This young fellah was in the office yesterday when I called.'

'It was Wednesday when you tapped on the window at me though; how did you know Simmonds was connected to Roz Sommerton if you didn't meet the student until Thursday?'

'I didn't. I just wanted to let you know I'd won, my body had turned up before you'd found your man.'

'OK. So the next day you came across this student, what did he tell you?'

'Well it was him and Simmonds's father really. You see, once the body had appeared I wasn't looking for a Miss Per any longer, I was tidying up after a suicide.'

'Assuming it *was* suicide.' said Reynard, 'not an 'accidental' or worse.'

'Nah, there's witnesses; two pensioners sitting in a shelter on the promenade eating their sandwich lunch saw him deliberately walk into the sea on Monday. The old man even tried to get to him to stop him, but the poor old beggar fell on the steps going down to the beach and by the time his wife had got him up the young fella had disappeared under the waves. No, it was suicide alright but until the body turned up it had to be treated as a Miss Per.'

'Right, so this student?

'Was in the office, for which he had a key. When I got there he didn't even know Simmonds was missing - as I said, he only comes in on Thursdays and Fridays. I was telling him Simmonds was dead when Simmonds's Dad arrived to do the same thing. He'd been informed when the body was found. It was *him* who told me about Roz Sommerton, and *him* who let me into Simmonds's flat, which is over the office.'

'Find anything?'

'Well I wasn't looking for anything really, except for another suicide note possibly, or something to explain why he'd gone off and topped himself, although now I know he was besotted by Roz Sommerton the note which we found in his pocket makes sense.'

'What did it say?'

'Not much. It only consisted of eight words 'Sorry Mum and Dad, I can't go on.'

Reynard dropped his hands and started rubbing his knees. 'I can't go on' It could mean anything.'

'Maybe she just given him the bullet; she did it regularly I believe.' said Best. 'And maybe he couldn't take it any more.'

'Right.' said Furness. 'Or perhaps she told him she was having someone else's baby … that would have got up his nose and could have pushed him over the edge to kill himself.'

'Or her.' suggested Groves.

Crowther got to his feet. 'I'm off, I've work to do.'

'Hang on Jack,' Reynard replied, relaxing his mode of address for a moment. 'This lot can get it all up on the board Sergeant Groves started the day before yesterday while you and I have a word with the Super about me taking on the 'Simmonds' file. If we don't volunteer it, he'll want to have his two penny worth anyway and God alone knows what way we'll wind up.'

Ten minutes later Reynard was back with Groves, Best, and Furness, who were sitting facing the incident board. He was positively beaming Simmonds is ours.' he said. 'So let's have a look at what we've got.'

Groves picked up a ruler and tapped the board. 'I'm trying your grid system this time, Guv,' she said, pointing to the pattern of lines dividing the board into columns of rectangular boxes. 'the names are across the top as you see, and the critical issues are written down the side. So, on the top, we have our five suspects: McCloskey, Papagos, Moss, Fogarty and Simmonds; and down the side we have Motive, Connection, Means, and Opportunity. Let's take them one at a time.

'Are you ruling out everyone else?' asked Best.

'Like who?'

'The soldier you were told about for a start, and the hotel manager Scott-Diggens, or one of her other rich 'clients'?'

'OK I'll put A. N. Other in the last box. Will that do for the moment? Fine so let's talk about McCloskey …'

Furness kicked off. 'I don't think it was him. I know there was the business of the car she sold him but it's the only connection we found between them. He's a bad 'un alright and I'm sure he was interfering with women he worked with and might even have raped them despite the fact the evidence on that score isn't strong but, as to killing Roz Sommerton … no, I don't think so. He's a 'No' as far as I'm concerned.'

'I agree,' said Best, 'he's a 'No' for me as well.'

'Guv?' said Groves who was putting crosses and ticks in the boxes as they went along.

'We're short of evidence because we've never caught up with him.' said Reynard. 'Even so, with no connection other than the car, no evidence of motive, and no obvious means or opportunity showing up, he's out. Unless you've seen something we haven't, Sergeant?'

'Which I haven't so …' she said, marking the boxes as each person spoke. 'OK so for McCloskey it's four ticks and twelve crosses. OK, now for Papagos.'

'Just a minute Sergeant,' said Reynard, we'll be here all day at this rate. Let's just go down the boxes and vote for 'em one at a time.'

'Fair enough.' she said, 'Papagos … Motive … D.C Furness?'

'Yes.'

'D.C. Best?'

'Yes.'

It took an hour at the end of which, undesirable as they were, McCloskey and Papagos had been ruled out as 'unlikely'; Moss and Fogarty were in as 'possible', as was Simmonds principally because of the question of motive, and A.N Other had been completely eliminated.

'So where do we go now Guv?' asked Groves.

'Well, we know where Doctor Moss is, he's in a cell at Steyning. We can charge him with obstructing the course of justice or wasting police time if we have to, though oddly enough I think he's actually happier in a cell, because of the remorse he has regarding not coming out in the open from the start. And we know where Fogarty is, and that there are charges pending which'll keep him behind bars for a while. So it just leaves Simmonds. Let's go to his apartment and his office, and see what we can find. I have the keys to both.'

218, Marine Road, Brighton Sussex.
Saturday 20th February 2010, 10.00 a.m.

The little row of six shops with living quarters above looks across Marine Road to the sea. It's about equidistant from Brighton Town Centre and Rottingdean and is surrounded by expensive houses most of which are lived in all year round, though some are holiday homes.

They tried the office first. The large-pane shop windows either side of the inset double entrance doors had been frosted to prevent people looking in. Even so it was bright inside despite the time of year. There were two architects' drawing boards, one inside each bay window, and a line of filing cabinets with wide drawers set back between a small washroom and a work table, which served as a desk.

The downstairs search didn't take long and they found nothing to connect Tony Simmonds and Roz Sommerton. However, upstairs they found plenty.

The first indication of Roz's recent presence in the flat was the ring - a gold one with a rose embossed on it, roughly as Marion had described. It was obviously the 'engagement' ring and it was lying on the table next to a pad of writing paper, the remaining sheets of which bore the same water mark, and were the same size as the note Sergeant Crowther had discovered in Simmonds's pocket. These two items alone would have been enough to tie Simmonds to Sommerton but there was more, there was a blood stain on the corner of the mantelpiece which they hoped would prove to be hers; and in the garage at the back of the premises was his car, a gun metal grey 2004 Hyundai Sante Fe 4x4 with a tyre pattern like the one they'd photographed in the car park near where they found the mitten. Under the front seat … was a single lady's red silk covered shoe.

The final item they discovered, one which they hoped would further prove Roz Sommerton had been in his car and that he'd been at the car park at Fyling Castle, was a pair of driving gloves found on the vehicle's front seat. The right hand one had a button missing, the left hand one hadn't and it bore the stamp of its maker 'Dent', like the one Geordie Hawkins had sieved from the snow covering Roz Sommerton's body.

As they went down the stairs Groves spotted a framed photograph hanging on the wall. It was of Simmonds, standing at barbecue and turning over a steak with a long handled fork. Written on the mount in a woman's handwriting she recognised as Roz's, was one word ... 'Chef'. She took it down off the wall and turned it over. On the back was written 'A memento for 'the chef' … thanks for a lovely birthday party. Roz'. 'So now we know 'Chef' was just a fun name she'd given him,' said Reynard, 'one he'd hung onto in the hope of prolonging their relationship.'

On the way back in car with all the damning evidence they'd collected they tried to work out exactly what had happened on the last night of Roz Sommerton's life. Reynard summed it up.

'So,' he said, 'it looks as though she met Simmonds by chance at the bottom of the steps of The Feathers Hotel when she ran out after the row with Papagos, and he drove her back to his flat ostensibly to comfort her but hoping to swing her back to him. At some stage he must have tried to persuade her to take the 'engagement' ring back, and she must have refused it. A struggle then probably broke out and somehow she fell and hit her head on the mantelpiece. When he realised she was dead he panicked … carried her out to his car and drove to the car park at Fyling Castle where he tried to hide her body in a snow drift. Then, the next day, full of remorse at what he'd done, he wrote the note, walked into the sea, and drowned himself.'

Groves, broke the silence which followed Reynard's conclusion. 'At the end of the day then Guv it wasn't such a complicated story after all.'

'No it wasn't.' said Reynard, 'And if Simmonds's body had been found the day he killed himself, and we'd got hold of the note which was in his pocket, we'd have had this all tied up by Wednesday.'

'Is that it then?' asked Best, looking at his watch and wondering if he'd get to the football ground in time for 'kick-off'.'.

'We'll put it to bed and *then* we'll go.' said Reynard. 'Don't worry it'll only take an hour.'

Sussex Police Major Incident Suite, Sussex House, Brighton Sussex. Saturday 20th February 2010. 12.10. p.m.

Reynard put down his mug, picked up a biscuit, and looked at it thoughtfully. Groves, Best, and Furness were sitting opposite to him, and recognising the signs knew they were in for a period of silence which they daren't risk breaking. Eventually he glanced up at them and smiled. 'Sorry, I was just going over it all again, in my mind.'

'A good result.' said Groves.

Best nodded 'Terrific.'

'Absolutely.' said Furness.

'I'm not so sure.' Reynard answered, first shaking his head then taking a bite out of the biscuit and showering his jacket with crumbs. 'Damn!'

Groves, ignoring the outburst seemed puzzled by Reynard's hesitancy. 'Come on Guv; wrapped up in a week's is pretty good isn't it.'

Reynard shook his head. 'It was all there from the start when you think about it. A young man who'd been engaged to her going and killing himself; no … we slipped up. We shouldn't have ignored what was obvious and rushed off to chase what looked interesting only to find it, had nothing to do with her death in the end.'

'You mean Dimitri Papagos and Co.' said Best.

'Yes … Papagos, McCloskey, Fogarty … even poor old Mossy. We should have thought it out more fully.' said the Reynard, picking two more crumbs off his lapel and dropping them one by one into the waste paper basket. 'The damned information was all there, pointing us in the right direction, and we ignored it. We should have looked for her fiancé the minute we heard about him.'

'We didn't recognise the information for what it was, you mean Guv, like a clue in a cryptic crossword puzzle.'

Reynard nodded. 'And I'm no good at them either. My wife does the one in the Telegraph every day, waltzes through it, but I can't understand the damned answers or match them to the clues even when she explains them to me. And look how long it took us to discover how like her mother Roz was.'

'In what respect?' asked Groves.

'In wanting a bespoke purpose made baby - a perfect child with no man attached.' he answered.

'Like the Lebensborn,' said Furness, 'I was reading about them recently - the perfect Aryan race the Nazis tried to create.'

'True.' said Groves, 'and, just as her mother picked Mossy's brother, Gerry; Roz picked Dimitri.'

'And look how livid he was when he realised how he'd been used.' said Reynard, rubbing his knees. 'We missed the point you see when we gave her the benefit of the doubt and said she was just fickle and flighty. She wasn't that at all - she was deliberating - looking for a perfect man. No we thought she'd been snuffed out in the prime of her life by some murdering bastard who was trying to take advantage of her. We never saw how she'd finally pushed one poor guy too far.'

Groves nodded. 'Or that what we saw as promiscuity was, in her case, a process of elimination - her way of working out who came up to scratch as far as fathering the child she wanted was concerned.'

'Even at the very last knocking we nearly got it wrong.' said Reynard.

'How come?'

'By reading Simmonds's suicide note incorrectly. We took it he'd committed suicide because he was upset at hearing of her death, not that he did it because he'd killed her. If we'd spotted the way she treated men generally, and him in particular … you know, 'engaged one minute and 'not engaged' the next, we might have worked out what he'd done and why he'd committed suicide. More coffee anyone?'

'I'll have drop Guv,' replied Best. What'll happen now? Will the case be closed?'

'Not until the inquest's over and we've convinced the coroner Simmonds murdered her, which looks very likely. After all we know the button came off his glove and the shoe turned up in his car, so if the DNA taken from the skin under her fingernail matches his, the case can be put to bed.'

'And Fogarty, Papagos and the others?'

'Fogarty'll be for the high jump - customs and excise will see to it. Papagos will patch things up with Scott-Diggens and they'll get on with their lives. McCloskey has disappeared and won't surface in this area again.'

'And Doctor Moss?'

'Ah, poor old Mossy, what a mess he's made of things, but oddly enough he's going to be better off than ever.'

'Because he's going back to a more tranquil life on the farm he's unexpectedly inherited.'

Reynard chuckled, 'Not on your life … he's selling it. And he'll make a bomb because of a new road they want to put through it. He rang me late last night to apologise again, and he told me all about it.'

'Will he come back to us d'you think?'

'No … he won't be able to and he doesn't want to; his doctoring is over, the GMC wouldn't countenance his leaving Charlotte Somerton on her kitchen floor while there was still a faint possibility she could have been revived. He'll be struck off if he doesn't resign.'

'Might she have recovered?' asked Best.

'Who knows?' Reynard replied, 'Anyway Mossy won't need his stethoscope where he's going. When the sale's gone through he and his wife are moving Cyprus.

Right, that's it, PharmoChem again on Monday … eight o'clock sharp. OK?'

'Of course, Governor.' they all replied.'

The towns, villages, and establishments
mentioned in this book
are a mix of the real and the imagined.
All the characters are fictitious.

Alan Grainger
2012

Once again I would like to thank
my friend and best-selling author,
David Rice,
for the encouragement
he has given me.

About the author

Alan Grainger is an Englishman who emigrated to Ireland at the time when everyone else seemed to be going the other way. He got seduced by the lifestyle, married an Irish woman and never went back. They have three children and seven grandchildren. His business career ended unexpectedly early when his company was taken over and a whole new world of opportunity opened up. Ever since then, other than when he's watching rugby or cricket, he has been travelling, painting, and writing. His journeys have taken him all over the world, provided him with much of the background material which features in his books, and allowed him to choose authentic sets against which he can tell his stories.

The following books written by the same author are available from Create Space, Amazon, and other major online retailers. They may also be obtained by ordering through any bookshop.

The Learning Curves

Divided from his father, and frozen out of his home in Ireland by his new stepmother, sixteen year old Jimmy O'Callaghan runs away, resolving never to return. With no one to guide and support him he finds himself with little option but to learn about life and love as best he can. He's aided in his quest for enlightenment, success, and happiness, by an unlikely collection of worldly people, the sort of people he would never have encountered, let alone befriend, at home in Templederry. Starting off with the few pounds he'd stolen from the till in his father's pub the night before he left, and with little appreciation of how big a risk he was taking, his personality and determination ensure nothing is beyond his reach.

This book is the first of The Templederry Trilogy, and is partly set in the rural Irish town of Templederry, County Tipperary. It is followed by Father Unknown and The Legacy

Father Unknown

The fragile and sometimes volatile relationship between two brothers, Dick and Roger Davenport, is demolished forever when they find out something previously unknown to them about their beginnings. In the aftermath of the violence which follows their discovery Dick, strongly supported by his grandfather Archie, sets off in a new direction; one which brings him to Ireland on a journey of more surprising discoveries.

This book is the second of The Templederry Trilogy. It is preceded by The Learning Curves and followed by The Legacy.

The Legacy

When an heir hunter turns up looking for Charlie Cassidy and finds he's been dead for years he tells Cassidy's son and daughter he has information which might connect them, through their late father, to an unclaimed legacy. He asks them if they'd like him to process their claim; but they think his fees are too high and decide to do the job themselves. It's a choice they regret when they discover their father was not the man they thought he was.

The Legacy is the third and last book of The Templederry Trilogy. It is preceded by The Learning Curves and Father Unknown

The same author's two other murder/mystery novels, featuring Detective Chief Inspector 'Foxy' Reynard, are available from Create Space, Amazon, and other on-line booksellers, or by ordering through bookshops.

Eddie's Penguin

When a young girl's quest to find the father she has never met becomes entangled in a police investigation into a series of seemingly unconnected murders she has no idea the information she digs up will ultimately lead to the uncovering of the last bit of the jigsaw the police are struggling to put together. Detective Chief Inspector 'Foxy' Reynard who makes his first appearance in this murder/mystery story leads the team from Sussex CID who ultimately solve the mystery and the crimes.

Deadly Darjeeling.

When Nelson Deep, a wealthy tea merchant, is found dead in his study in bizarre circumstances and Detective Chief Inspector 'Foxy' Reynard is called in, a solution seems inevitable. Such an assumption however, makes little allowance for the dysfunctional and self-centred attitudes the D.C.I. uncovers as he attempts to unravel the strange relationships

Alan Grainger's spy thriller/saga Blood On The Stones is also available from and Create Space, Amazon, and other on line booksellers and bookshops.

It's the story of two young men, once close as brothers, who fall out over a girl when they are in their twenties and go their separate ways. Their vow 'never to meet again' is forgotten though, when they find themselves face to face in the course of an attempted royal assassination.

All books by this author are now available in e-book format and may be obtained from stockists of electronic books all over the world.

13373709R00147

Made in the USA
Charleston, SC
05 July 2012